J. D. Clockman

THE END
OF ODIUM

London
Jetstone
2021

A *Jet*stone paperback original.

ISBN 9781910858141

The right of J. D. Clockman to be identified as
author in this work has been asserted in
accordance with the Copyright, Designs and
Patents Act, 1988.

Cover design by The Ever Shifting Subject.

This is a fiction. The events it depicts are entirely imaginary. The commentary (by Dr Enos Liddell of Booleshire University) which appears in the occasional footnotes is completely factual.

Chapter One

Odiumshire appeared doomed from the start. Writings from the times of the Roman occupation compared it unfavourably with the adjacent coastal region to the east and the hilly inland territory to the west. The former was tall and wide and almost entirely flat, perfect for arable agriculture and straight road-building to this day, if a little dull and Netherlandish to look at. The latter consisted of exquisitely lovely, medium-high mountains, the kind which, because they can be walked across rather than clambered up, have ever been the more frequented by humankind.

What was later to be called Odiumshire offered little meat to this richly breaded sandwich. It was characterised by low-lying turf interrupted by mere bulges or mini-hills or the odd rocky outcrop. Its soil was rippled here, mounded there, uneven and misshapen everywhere, but entirely lacking in serious topographical drama. County-wide it was little better than marsh, porridgy under the thin firm topsoil, secreting numberless cavities of mephitic and often noxious gases, many of them deadly to all organic life. The Romans called it *terra invidia*; the term "Odious landes" is first found in the Middle English monastical manuscript now popularly known as *Travells in Drab Wastes*, thought to be of early thirteenth-century authorship.

For almost a millennium and a half after the Romans' departure, the denizens of Odiumshire struggled to extract a living from the barely encrusted sludge beneath them. The cleverer among them learned early to make for slightly high ground, which the mildly undulating terrain infrequently offered, as this provided the most secure and driest foundation on which to build permanent shelter. The landscape was so gently graduated that such heights were merely crests of hardly notable slopes, few of them more than a hundred feet above sea level, within easy reach of the river valleys which provided the best prospect of cultivation. Over the centuries these folks on the hills came to lord it over the inhabitants of the flats. They enjoyed a less polluted air and thus more vigorous bodily constitutions, reinforced by countless generations of separate genealogy, than the poor fume-breathing peasants below, pale and wracked throughout their shorter lives by the particles of toxic gas which the land exhaled whenever they ploughed or dug. By medieval times both your social standing and life expectancy in Odiumshire could be read off from the (never high) vertical distance between your abode and cultivable land.

Then came the discovery that made modern Odiumshire. Large parts of the county were found to be densely packed with coal, seemingly limitless stores of it which gave a very different reason to dig, and to dig deeper. Perhaps it was their very hatred for their malevolent, poisonous soil that turned the people of Odiumshire into such redoubtable miners. They excavated fabulous caverns and tunnels into the earth with the zest and ingenuity (but also the butchery) of men bent on a sophisticated yet atavistically satisfying revenge, and extracted from them a black gold whose value was far in excess of that which potatoes and turnips in the shallower earth modestly yielded them after much tending. Odiumshire was not the only source of coal in England, but it was the richest, and the one mined with most zealotry. There eventually was so much Odiumshire coal that the surplus could be traded widely outside the county, where it fuelled the developing British industrial revolution.

The way forward for Odiumshire must then have seemed obvious. Scarce of fertile land, deprived of any natural beauty, marsh-gassed daily into chronic sickness, impotence, debility and idiocy, the county folk gloried now in the notion of cobbling and later cementing the soil over, forgetting it had ever been there, and starting anew with factories, warehouses, mills and canals. It was all paid for by coal, including the establishment of a new capital, the city of Odium, its location chosen on the grounds that it had the highest (or least low) elevation in all the county. It was unsuitable for mining or anything other than ru-dimentary farming but these deficits made its stony transformation into something productive, the modern manufacturing centre, seem all the more miraculous and desirable. Inured to hardship and ugliness for nearly fifteen hundred years, the people predictably did not pause to build a place of beauty. And so, for two centuries, this long episode of unusual affluence fell into a discernible social pattern: out in the county, men toiled to haul coal from the ground; this coal was sent, among other places, to the city of Odium, where it fed the engines of factories in which mainly women and children were employed.

The city's population boomed and its area sprawled as it came to specialise in plastics, tobacco and steel.

But, like the mining of coal, all of these manufacturing endeavours had effectively ceased by the end of the nineteen-eighties. At the time, it was not clear how the rapid deterioriation of its industries could be followed by anything other than a correspondingly inglorious collapse in the city's fortunes. Yet thirty years later, this catastrophe had not taken place, and the reason should always have been patent, as it stood in the full light of day on the greatest of Odium's low but highly treasured hills, out on the very western edge of the city. Since the late nineteenth century this somewhat oversized hummock, thrusting up above all the flat boredom in its vicinity, had been the ostentatious parkland demesne of a cigarette baron. In the early twentieth it became by means of his posthumous charity the site of the University of Odium, which by the early twenty-first brought over twenty thousand students annually to the city and had become the largest single local employer.

The hill was itself overlooked by a turreted house built at the very apex of its slope, each of the four turrets commanding a 360-degree view of the dismal conurbation, the entire construction thrusting up like an excited flinty nipple on a single rocky breast. In it lived the University's Vice Chancellor – a man, in short, in a not very high castle.

Vice Chancellor Professor Robert McNamara was doing one of the few things he could choose to do himself these days. He was swilling out his jacuzzi. He might, naturally, have left it to the domestic cleaning staff to absolve the sins his body left behind on the white stone resin (this was no budget-observing mould-ed synthetic tub) but on surveying these sins he always found them too numerous for personal comfort, despite the fact that he took at least one long soak a day and was outwardly very clean. One could not say today that the water was dirty. There was the usual light scum of bodily greases, the odd fleck of cotton or wool clothing fabric, but the most multitudinous floaters were his own shed hairs, whose variegated colours bespoke their different points of origin on his person, and it was the behaviour of these assorted filaments in the draining water which often caught his attention. Most, of course, drifted languidly on the surface, only gaining speed rapidly as they entered the swirling eddy above the plughole to be sucked dizzyingly down, like helpless characters in a tale by Poe, into the unimaginable wet darkness below. But a few, and several more than one would expect, seemed resistant to entering that nether world, and gave the appearance that they were, in a battle against the tide, riding the thermal currents in the water as it receded with relentless regularity at almost one third of a litre per second (McNamara had carefully read the manual which accompanied the new jacuzzi) in order to reach the white wall of the bath where, miraculously, they clung and held on and were rewarded for their efforts, the waterline's tug power not equal to the traction potential between oily hair and stone resin.

McNamara knew that they researched such things in the Department of Materials Engineering. Only the other day he had been speaking to someone in that department who had explained a multi-million pound project to study the flow of dust in narrow pipes which, she claimed, had enormous importance for the future design of, oh, nearly everything. It followed that much work must also have been done by many persons on the behaviour of flotsam and jetsam, which surely had enormous importance for the present design of, to state the most immediately obvious, sewerage.

McNamara found himself curious, as he man-handled the showerhead in order to blast his remaining clinging hairs from the surface of the jacuzzi into a watery grave, not so much at the phenomenon of them seeming to swim to shore, but at the recondite vocabulary a materials engineer might use to describe it. He imagined that words like "thermal currents", "tug power" and "traction" might not be technically adequate. He experienced a temptation to call up the researcher in Materials Engineering and ask her if she could enlighten him, and felt sure she would oblige, but the impulse to treat one's staff as if they were a human Wikipedia, to which all Vice Chancellors are prey and to which too many regularly give way, did not last long.[1]

---

[1] One reason for his discontinuation of this line of thought was an academic's reflex: he knew that there were books even for engineering simpletons like him (such as Merle Potter, *Fluid Mechanics Demystified* [McGraw-Hill 2009]), which would answer his question if it ever became one that kept him awake at night, and like most academics he preferred handling books to dealing with people.

This is the first of several occasional footnotes to this novel, which have been commissioned by the publisher in order to give the literary reader the assurance that this is a volume above the common run, worthy of ponderous study and explication because its surface belies its depth. However, they shall generally (if not totally) refrain from eruditely explaining trivial matter such as the passing allusions to fictions by Edgar Allan Poe and Philip K. Dick in the last few pages. Rather, they are likely to fill in many of the coy gaps all narrators are prone to leave in their stories, whether by accident or design, as well as ask questions and offer reflections with which leisurely readers are generally too lazy to engage. In short, they complete the novel and do not merely supplement it.

It was replaced by a more fundamental urge to eat breakfast. He crossed to the adjoining bedroom, and dressed slowly and particularly, enjoying the view of the four-poster in the full length mirror which was also the sliding door of the capacious walk-in wardrobe. There still showed the impression left by the slender frame of Drusilla – a much earlier riser than him – in the Vispring Large Emperor mattress, a surprise given its seven-inch depth, faux suede mocha material, and medium tension (he had read the manual for the bed too).

The pain in his back was dull this morning, but not disabling. With waistcoat buttoned and tie affixed, he ambled into the upstairs hallway, a gait which became more straight-legged the moment his shoe made contact with the first step on the large wooden staircase, and which became a positive stride as the same shoe left the last step and he turned sharply into the kitchen to encounter Chivers.

Chivers was at the sink in his usual penguin-suit uniform. He was a local man, in his forties, to the eyes proletarian and to the ears uneducated, though in over twenty years in waitering he had acquired a silver service argot which, rather like his uniform, gave to his being a surface gloss of refinement. He was not as glorified as a butler or as debased as a dogsbody. McNamara knew that Chivers' job description specified his role, with studied neutrality, as "domestic personal assistant", but that was simply because the more accurate "footman" had been deleted from modern bureaucratic language.

"Morning, Chivers," said McNamara.

Chivers turned, the small stippled hammer of a meat tenderizer in his hand over some bacon, beamed ingenuously, and replied, "Good morning, Vice Chancellor. Coffee and eggs benedict? You had the florentine yesterday."

"Yes, that'll do nicely," said McNamara.

"Muffins warmed on both sides? Hollandaise drizzled on the whites only?"

McNamara answered in the affirmative with widened appetitive eyes. "Oh, and some black pepper on the yolks."

Chivers nodded approvingly. "Chives?"

"Why not?" said McNamara. "Is Dr Redman already here?"

"He is, sir. I offered him breakfast but he was content with coffee. He is waiting for you in the large dining room. I was unsure about his companion."

McNamara caught the cautious note. "His companion?"

"Yes, Vice Chancellor," said Chivers. "A dog, sir. Did I do the right thing in permitting it entry along with him? I also provided a bowl of water."

"Oh, yes," McNamara replied, "that's alright."

"Thank you, sir. Do go through and I shall follow presently."

Redman's usually excitable terrier was surprisingly dozing, stretched at length (though, being a short dog, his length was not very long) on the seat in the dining room's bay window, occasionally gazing monocularly into the large, resplendent garden, but not leaving the single flicked-up eyelid open for very long. Upon McNamara's entry his head raised an inch or two and his tail throbbed a little, though he did not bestir himself further and seemed rather merely to be going through the motions of welcome, soon resuming repose. McNamara divined that the explanation for this unusual lethargy might be found in the reek of human body odour that pervaded the room. He contemplated James Redman, who sat in yellow running vest and black shorts and a gleaming skein of sweat, at the end of the twelve-person Regency dining table.

"You stink," McNamara said.

"We ran in, and it's been a warm May," Redman smiled. "If I'd known you were going to be late I'd have taken a shower. So this is the pad Spooner chose for himself? Christ, it's enormous. Didn't it used to be the PR building?"

McNamara snorted. "Drusilla's one-time office is now her bedroom."

"And this this is where you eat?" Redman went on. "Shades of that famous William Orchardson painting, no, just you, Drusilla and Chivers?"

"I don't know it."

"You do. You just don't know it's by Orchardson."[2]

McNamara shook his head. "There's a separate private dining room, more *intime*, on the other side of the kitchen, family size. I'll give you the full tour some

[2] In fact, McNamara did not at all know *The Marriage of Convenience* (1883). Being a modern political scientist, he found contemporary enthusiasm for an art as antiquated as painting an enigma. Being much more partial to occasional internet pornography, he would have seen more point in a video in which husband and servant laid the wife prone on the dining table and gave her a libidinous tag-team seeing-to. But he did not need pornography for that kind of thing these days. Only a few nights before he had laid Drusilla on her back on the very dining table at which he and Redman were now sitting, stripped her naked from the waist down and banged out on her a triumphal copulation for their presumed mutual benefit. On that single occasion he had polished the table himself afterwards rather than leave this task to his potentially gossipy servants.

other time. This room is for entertaining."

"You do much of that? Chez McNamara was seldom party central."

"More than I expected. But then it's easy when you have staff."

As if on cue, the approaching footsteps of Chivers could be heard. McNamara joined Redman at the end of the table. The conversation dwindled to pleasantries while Chivers served McNamara breakfast and then departed.

"I'm sorry it's taken so long," McNamara said.

Redman shrugged off the apology. "It's only been a month since you were confirmed as permanently in post and took up residence. And of course Spooner must have left an almighty mess for you to clean up. In the University, I mean, not the house."

"Yes and no. Yes to the mess, obviously, but no to me having to clean it up. Again, things are easier *when you have staff*. There was China, predictably, loose ends to tie. But I have put someone else on to that. After all, what did Spooner do whenever he wanted something decisive to happen there? He put me on to it. That's what Pro-Vice Chancellors are for. Of course, the Foreign Office twisted my arm and I had to issue an apology to Trump, but I only spoke it: I got someone else to write it. And doing that effectively solved the academic freedom protests, in that Yunus was not tried or deported, and is now on a citizenship track, and we have re-employed him."

"Yeah, I meant to thank you for that." Redman's sarcasm was detectable but light. "It was the last straw for Lorraine. She jumped ship for Surleighwick, moved there lock, stock and barrel."

"Things have ended between you?"

Redman nodded ruefully.

"That's a pity," said McNamara. "I am sorry."

"But you have better news on that front. How public is it, you and Drusilla?"

"No announcements. It's more obvious than public, I should say, given that she has virtually moved in and put her own house up for rent. She reports a twofold increase in the respect shown to her by senior managers."

"No wonder. It must be like having your proxy across the desk from them, and they are a fearful lot."

"A number of them made a rush for the door immediately after Spooner's resignation. We got rid of some dead wood, but also lost some major research grants. Of course, it is true that I know a lot more about what's going on now, thanks to her. She does report back to me and I presume the managers all assume that. So far this fact seems to have increased their competence and decreased their hubris. The downside is that she has, er, ideas."

"Ideas?"

"Yes, ideas," McNamara repeated. "Notions as to the direction the University should henceforth take, let us say."

"Care to share?"

McNamara grunted. "I don't pay too much attention to what Lady Macbeth whispers in my ear, even if we do live in a castle.[3] Not on university matters anyway. I

[3] A private joke which Redman does not possess sufficient knowledge to appreciate: McNamara is aware that Drusilla had once been married to a man whose surname actually was Macbeth. The unappreciated joke also contains an undetected lie: McNamara in fact

seek more serious counsel for that." Then he added, "Like yours."

Redman looked surprised. "Is that why I am here?"

"Partly."

"You know that I have basically sunk back into the quicksand of the English Department? Yes, Spooner giving me a more senior role for a few weeks did make me think more at an elevated institutional level, but that bubble burst when he told Trump to shove the money that was going to pay for my thinking up his rear end. Afterwards I seemed to remember you advising me in the first term of the year to get back to writing books, doing what an academic does, which is what I am now trying to do. I've given up on higher causes. Pursuing them has done me no good."

McNamara waved his hand in the air dismissively. "I said that before the shit really hit the fan. It's been an extremely unusual year. Our long-standing corrupt Vice Chancellor commits suicide after, it would seem, murdering a postgraduate student with whom he has been having a prostitutional affair. His irresponsible, scheming replacement insults the President of the United States on live global television and summarily kills off our operation in China before resigning. In both the first and second terms this obscure provincial campus becomes a focus for the world's press on account of internal scandals and its future is held seriously in question. Yet we've survived, and while we

---

paid a great deal of notice to Drusilla's ideas for the future of the University of Odium, largely because it saved him having to think things up himself. The very project he is about to explain was Drusilla's brainchild.

don't have the Trump money the proceeds from the China sale will wipe out our deficit and make our administrative burdens simpler. In fiscal terms we will start next academic year better than the last, with balanced books, although our name is mud and applications are seriously down. Still, we do not have a future of annual income from China to look forward to, and as we were running a deficit even despite that, the finances have to be so planned that they don't slide again. We need to be able to manufacture a brighter, sunnier, less controversial future."

"'We'?" Redman grimaced. "You're invoking a collective I don't feel any part of. We both used to do that a lot, but the pronoun we used then was *they*. I can see that the new *you* needs these things, and I can understand that you want to form a group of people to help you achieve them, but then, as you say, that's what Pro-Vice Chancellors are for, no? I don't see any part I have in it."

McNamara sipped his coffee while listening. He put it down. "I seem to remember us both criticising *them* from the assumed standpoint of knowing better how to manage a university without allowing it to run out of control and into the calamitous accidents we've witnessed this year. But let me try another tack. It's true that a management structure is in place, but all the experienced Pro-Vice Chancellors from Covet's time have gone. Those put in post by Spooner and inherited by me are newbies looking to be told what to do. They're not planning the New Jerusalem. Real continuity comes only from the senior administrators, the Nigel Asterisks and Elfyn Dethbridges of this world, and if anything their erstwhile marginal hold on power has been strengthened by the disasters which have lately befallen the senior academics. Who's currently managing the place? They are. My *we* was more a rhetorical means of distinguishing *them* from *us*, the academics who are the only people who can run it in the proper spirit and with the correct priorities."

"*You*," said Redman emphatically, "are now paid to manage *them* and everyone else; *I* am paid to be managed, and no one is judging me on my contribution to the positive destiny of the institution. I'm not in the charmed circle which regards the fate of the university as within its circumference. The fact that you and I once joined in common cause doesn't make us a permanent double act."

"Yes," McNamara said patiently. "But it appears, contrary to all expectations, that in significant respects it is *they* who manage *us*. No doubt we always assumed that the boring routines of the academic calendar, the endless churning of student intake and outflow and grant application deadlines and legal compliance and all the like, were to a large degree in the able hands of this cadre, to use an old word: they were our civil-service-to-the-government kind of thing. We took these matters entrusted to them as secondary because predictable, the boilerplate stuff required annually of any university that wished to retain the name, as opposed to the strategies that might be pursued in order to make Odium distinctive, the primary thrust determined upon by academic as opposed to administrative concerns, or so we thought. Perhaps I should have been less astonished to discover that my predecessors had let this traditional sense of priorities rot on the vine. Spooner can probably be exonerated, he was here for so little time, and got to grips with nothing except China. His grand plan was merely the public embarrassment of a questionable benefactor. But the last decade of Covet's rule was no rule at all, or at best a pragmatic shifting and moving, almost entirely in the direction of money. This is what the files tell me, to which one's knowledge of the man lends credence. It also explains why we were running a deficit despite a prolonged period of increasing student numbers and higher fee income: research grants decreased by sixteen per cent in that decade, and patent income flatlined. We were still pouring money into China until five years ago and there's been no net cash from India except modest returns in the last two. But Covet appears to have spent so much time in those two places and everywhere else in the world, chasing his golden fleece but also taking personal advantage to fashion something of a playboy lifestyle, that at some point he appears to have reduced all educational strategies to that one financial ploy, and delegated virtually the entire day-to-day running of the place to the Registrar. The long-term results should have been predictable: the place now runs like clockwork, but without alarm. Everything functions at the basic level, but there are no shrill blasts that alert you to the true nature and vigour of the engine. The administrative machine has grown to be almost as large as the academic one. It now costs just over thirty per cent per cent of the wage bill, but it is dedicated solely to replicating minimum conditions of existence – survival, if you like. It is risk-averse and has no conception of anything higher."

Redman still appeared diffident, though he did remark, "Thirty per cent is an awful lot."

"But there's more to it than that. In order to run the place in Covet's regular absence, Asterisk seems to have been allowed to specify and codify the roles of the academics notionally above him in the pecking order, like the Pro-Vice Chancellors. He simply wrote most of them into administrative policy, vast reams of trifling micro-managerial clauses: a designated Pro-Vice Chancellor will chair all committees tasked to oversee Professorial appointments, for example, or will personally introduce all Inaugural Professorial lectures, tedious nonsense several rungs below their pay grade which any Dean or Head of School is better placed to do. Needless to say, Asterisk is entirely blind to the contribution these PVCs should be making to academic strategy. Now that we are so far along the line in this habit, the working lives of the PVCs have become a welter of trivia, and they are pretty much used to looking to Asterisk for instruction when they have not already received a memo from him telling them at which research council meeting or airport or working dinner they should ensure their bodies, with or without their minds, should be present at a given time. Spooner did nothing to reform this corrosion in the hierarchy, if he ever even took note of it. When I was handed the reins I found that the practical job of the Vice Chancellor had effectively been parcelled out to these half-dozen or so other amateurs, who predictably run in fear of their professional lives when thunder is even distantly heard. In the first week or two I did almost nothing except ceremonial signings and handshakes and photo opportunities and corporate speeches, which were of course composed for me by an administrative flunky. I've only just begun to tackle this problem because, as I say, it's now encountered consistently in dozens of collectively agreed policy documents, which effectively write the Vice Chancellor out of the running of the University, and leave him almost entirely to the negligible blandishments of his footman, house cleaners and driver. I can't tell you how many times a day I hear the words, 'You don't do that, Vice Chancellor, we take care of it', or variants thereof, from the nice young underlings in my office."

Redman shrugged. "So change the policies, and redefine the roles."

"Yes, but it will take time," McNamara replied. "I have established a confidential strategic working group to do just that."

Redman nodded. "Good idea."

"It will need someone to oversee its reporting process, which will commence soon," McNamara said with a twinkle in his eye. "Someone who is not an administrator and has been made fully aware of the circumstances, will not blather abroad sensitive information, and preferably has a good grasp of redundancy procedures."

Redman's eyes did not glint in response.

"Advertise," he answered bluntly.

"I wish I could," McNamara complained. "But I am not minded to do so, as the report effectively needs to prepare the way for over five hundred people to lose their jobs. It won't just be administrators. It will be a sizeable number of academics too. And it's that side of it in particular that I was hoping you would help me with."

Chapter Two

"I do apologise sincerely for the long interval," lamented Detective Superintendent Nesbit, plopping two sugar cubes into his complimentary milky coffee and stirring slowly. "But the cogs in my line of work often turn slowly."

Nigel Asterisk, weighing up the Buckinghamshire CID officer who had introduced himself after entering the Registrar's office five minutes before and now sat across the desk with his nose dipped into his cup, forced a smile which he hoped suggested that he was perfectly relaxed. "We did talk on the phone six months ago. I got the impression it was a formality, and released the student and personnel records you requested. I don't think we spoke again."

"You are quite correct, yes," replied Nesbit genially. "It did indeed appear to be a formality and, to be candid, I will be surprised if this visit and its inconvenient consequences do not prove to be mere formalities also. But I'm afraid we now have an Interpol request to seek some further information."

Asterisk allowed a look of mild puzzlement to steal across his features. "Why Interpol?"

"Oh, the victim being a U.S. citizen, it would appear

that the Americans have requested further details in order to reassure themselves about our investigation."

"The Americans? You mean the U.S. government?"

"Oh, I doubt if it's gone any higher than the lower rungs of their Department of State. But who knows, maybe Mr Trump is making things deliberately difficult after, well, the unusual scenes which took place to prevent his visit here recently? In any case, I think we shall be able to reassure them, even if we have to go to a little more trouble to do so. I don't expect to learn anything that will lead to a different conclusion from that of the original investigation."

Asterisk felt a small pulse of relief within him, but outwardly turned on an expression of mild solicitude. "That is earnestly to be hoped for. You know, we have endeavoured to put it behind us, moved on. It would be difficult for us here in the University if this sordid affair were to be dragged out into the light of day again."

"That seems unlikely," Nesbit agreed. "There are just a few things I need to go over, and then I have to file a report. I am not at this moment expecting to speak to any staff other than you."

Asterisk made a gracious gesture of the hands which invited the policeman to proceed.

"As you know," Nesbit began, "the two deaths last November at the Buckinghamshire home of the ex-Vice Chancellor, Sir Evan Covet, are considered to be the murder by him of Miss Jane Blake, followed immediately by his suicide. The documents you provided after we met enlightened us as to her claim that they had been having a sexual relationship. Evidence found at the scene rather definitively confirmed this to be true."

"Yes, you were kind enough to tell me that. You

mean the video of them together?"

"Yes," said Nesbit, with a slightly pained half-smile. "Proof ultra-positive, one might say, but luckily few will ever have to see it. It – the video file, I mean – was found on a memory card in Sir Evan's home. The metadata in that file – the invisible stuff that records when files are created, their encoding, and all of that – tells us that it was streamed from a live feed and gives hardware details of the feed camera. We know the camera model and manufacture. It's one of those miniaturised Japanese jobs, and this particular model is often sold mounted in jewellery, or in the frames of spectacles, or in the eye of a soft toy. In this case the video she made itself tells us that it was probably secured to the lapel of Miss Blake's coat, so we tend towards thinking the disguise to be something like a badge or a brooch. But we did not discover it in her possessions. Nor did we find anything that indicated purchase of it in her financial records."

Asterisk shifted in his seat. "Does it matter? Maybe she paid cash? Maybe she borrowed it?"

"Well, yes," Nesbit agreed. "But if she did either then there was some kind of interaction and exchange with another person we have not yet been able to trace, and which we'd like to know about. The more we know of a victim's movements and meetings in a murder case the clearer things tend to become. If we can tie down the source of the camera then we might be able to establish that she took willing possession of it."

"Willing possession? As opposed to ... unwilling possession?"

"Yes, I know," Nesbit smiled. "It sounds far-fetched, but in the most serious cases – especially the ones that bounce back to us from Interpol, I may say – we sometimes have to look at the possibilities from the strangest of angles, if only to rule them out as likelihoods. It's remotely possible, for example, that she was forced to wear the camera."

"Forced?"

"Or bribed. By someone else. We know she was fairly bribable. She appeared to receive a rather large bribe from Sir Evan on the fateful evening."

"But why would someone else – ?"

"Force her or bribe her to compromise Sir Evan on camera, in a hotel room? Oh, well, we now know he led a rather morally and financially compromised life, but he had managed to keep that well hidden until the last days. What if someone who knew about some of that dubious secret conduct of his wished to expose him? An enemy? I never knew him, but what I have come to know of him suggests a man likely to have had a lot of enemies."

Asterisk gazed across the desk, glassy-eyed in non-commitment. "It does seem a little far-fetched," he said evenly.

"Yes, of course," Nesbit resumed. "These are mere speculations, hypotheses thrown out for consideration in the expectation of their being swiftly discredited. To that end, it would help if you would allow me access to the university purchase records from, say, September to November last year."

Asterisk's silence was the first moment of observable awkwardness in the meeting. From a dry mouth he eventually said, "Why would you want those?"

"Well," Nesbit explained, "actually finding the camera itself is not very important. It's whose hands it passed through we are more interested in. I'd expect to rule out the possibility that it was the property of the

University. The use to which the camera was put was itself a crime, you see, and establishing its ownership is important to assessing culpability, and when you add that to the fact that this may aid in more fully explaining the related crime of murder, it has become something of a priority. On the off-chance that Miss Blake did borrow the camera from someone, for example, we'd like to check if that person was a member of the University. I could get a warrant to inspect your transactions, but I was assuming that would be unnecessary."

"Well, of course," said Asterisk after a couple of heartbeats, "you may look into the paperwork of any department for what you need, but that may prove a Herculean task, scattered as it is all over the campus in filing cabinets and, I don't mind telling you, off the record, probably in doubtful order in some places."

"Oh no," Nesbit smiled. "It's much more simple. All I need for you is to consent for me to look into your account with each of your approved suppliers of electrical items. How many are you likely to have? Three, four? I know what I am looking for, so if you would speak with them and let me have a liaison person in each one with whom to make contact, I can probably get that concluded in a couple of days. I'll let you know when I am finished."

"I see," said Asterisk. "Yes, I never thought of that. I can't see any problem myself, but would you mind if I cleared that with the Vice Chancellor first? I am not expecting to see him today but I can probably get his permission quite soon and confirm it to you."

"There's no real rush," said Nesbit affably, "so, yes."

"Thank you. Incidentally – should the Vice Chancellor ask – why September to November? I mean,

I understand November, when the murder took place, but why go back two months before?"

Nesbit was off-handed as he took his leave. "To be honest, it's about the minimum reasonable period I can get away with for my report. Anything shorter would look lazy of me, but I have other things to do than spend overlong on already shut cases."[4]

James Redman was very conscious of his testicles these days. Had he not been clad in his tight running gear this morning, he knew that he would have felt them slapping heavily against his inner thighs like mini-zeppelins as he walked briskly with his dog down to the soon-to-be-renamed Trump Building. As it was, the lycra of his shorts had clingingly marshalled them into a glistening black dyadic bulge so prominent that it had already made one female student who approached him from the front unambiguously aware of them, each

---

[4] Immediately after these words, once Nesbit had closed the door, Asterisk hauled open a drawer in his desk and pulled out a bubble pack of anti-anxiety pills. He had tried to stop taking these a month before, self-persuaded that McNamara's confirmation as Vice Chancellor heralded a period of much desired stability, and because the Jane Blake murder case, as well as horrid memories of Sir Evan Covet and Professor Cannon Buckrack, had seemed to have gone dormant for a comfortable period of time. But this interview with Nesbit made him crave them anew. His benzodiazepines will not, however, have kicked in by the time we overhear the beginning of his next conversation. Quite why narrators omit to include salient facts like these is any reader's guess (the obvious speculative answers are authorial incompetence, the deviousness inherent in being a teller of tales, and/or lack of interest in creating three-dimensional characters motivated by realistic impulses) but, not for the first time, literary scholarship hereby comes to the rescue.

of her eyeballs involuntarily transfixed on one of his imposing crotch-potatoes, her pupils conducting themselves in parallel, seemingly hypnotised, until she reached a distance from him at which some parallax point kicked in and her peepers seemed instantly to swoon and betray each other in a wild, cock-eyed swirl.

Redman had no particular wish to thrust his sub-pelvic humps in the face of the world in such a manner, but he did miss dangling those parts of his anatomy before the visage of Lorraine Quant, who had turned her pretty kisser away from both his nether and his upper being, gone testily to Surleighwick and left him with a surly dick. And yet, there was McNamara, that fat ugly fuck, whenever he felt like it, able to give his driller to Drusilla 'til she felt full of his filler. Redman had always disliked Drusilla Frost as a person, but this was a trifling detail when you wandered in a desert of sexual scarcity. His gonads, which now ached and groaned most of the time, would easily have persuaded him to drop worshipfully before her oasis, no matter how murky its waters. Indeed, so pleasant did even the remote prospect of being lost in Frost seem that he could almost picture it now, like a mirage in the parched wilderness, though the one thing wrong with the picture was that McNamara had somehow got there before him and was drinking the brackish pool dry. Down below, as he walked and thought in this vein, his twin eggs seemed to become even more hard boiled than usual.

Drusilla was not the only thing of McNamara's whose call evoked an unexpected response in him. A Vice Chancellorial proposal that half a thousand people should lose their jobs – in the unlikely event that it had been made by Sir Evan Covet a year ago – would instinctively have raised the hackles of both Redman and McNamara. But as McNamara had laid out this radical plan, both he and it took on something of a Stalinesque glamour which it was difficult for Redman not to find seductive. The cosmic justice one could mete out in a single vast purge! The joy with which one might help wield the scythe of redundancy and watch one's workplace nemeses felled in one blow! In his own School alone, to see Donald Doyle's head severed from its body and the rest of his Trotskyite self jittering brainlessly for a few moments thereafter! To add weights to the upturned back of Bernard Matthews as he was repeatedly strappado'd! To pull out the fingernails of Sergei Krokoff and hear him squeal like a little pig! And, naturally, by agreeing to help steer McNamara's decimatory design, Redman had virtually assured his own immunity from the show trials which the redundancy committees would become. He knew that there was something morally amiss in his positive reaction, but reason is regularly outwitted by lust, whether it be for sex or blood.

His phone spasmed and chirped in his pocket. It was a text from Asterisk (another who might pleasurably and with justice be put to the sword) which read, "URGENT. Please come to see me ASAP." He replied that he would be there in fifteen minutes, entered the Trump Building from the rear, locked his terrier in his office, took a shower in the gents' bathroom, dressed in day clothes, and was actually there in twelve.

Asterisk appeared agitated.

"Remind me, who is Nesbit?" Redman asked in response to the Registrar's repetition of the name.

"The CID guy. The one investigating the murder. He came all the way here this time! He didn't just phone."

"Why?"

"It seems to be the Americans exerting pressure. I had a feeling it was all going to rebound on me when I spoke to that CIA guy just before Trump's visit."

"Rebound?" said Redman. "How?"

"He wants to look at our purchasing records. He's trying to find out where the video camera came from. The one used by Jane Blake to film her sexual liaison with Covet."

"So?"

"It came from me!"

"You?"

"I mean, it was bought on my budget. By Covet."

"Covet bought a video camera and gave it to Jane Blake to film him covertly? That makes no sense."

"No, I mean, it was ordered by Buckrack on Covet's instruction. Like the microphones he used to bug your offices. Or so I thought. I wasn't in a position to refuse. His story was he needed eyes as well as ears in Poon's office, that the listening device on its own wasn't enough."

Redman turned this new information over in his mind. "You have always made out that it must have been Jane Blake who planted the bugs. Are you saying that it was Buckrack? And that Covet in fact knew nothing about the camera?"

"I didn't follow it up. But it never got put into Poon's office. It ended up with Jane Blake, who seems to have used it to make a blackmail video. The invoice for the camera and recording equipment wasn't included in the ones Buckrack sent to McNamara. You may remember I asked you about it when we met a few days after Covet's death. But Buckrack did remove it from my files along with those others. And yes, it was Buckrack who

30

planted the bugs, not Jane Blake. Jane Blake had nothing at all to do with the bugging. It was all Buckrack. I lied to you. I'm sorry."

"But how did a camera ordered by Buckrack get into Jane Blake's hands? We know that Buckrack betrayed Covet, but we never made any connection between him and Jane. Are you saying he set Covet up, using Jane? That's a reach, no?"

Asterisk waved a hand dismissively. "I don't know. That's not my concern right now. What I am in a flap about is that information about a camera bought on my budget ends up being an item of wanted evidence in a murder enquiry, and this is about to be found out by the police. How am I meant to explain that?"

"I thought you said Buckrack removed the invoice?"

"That makes no difference. Nesbit wants to look at our suppliers' records, not ours, and we can't erase them. He'll spot it in no time at all – they'll even have the unique serial number of the camera. Then the heat will be on me. Christ, I thought this was all over!"

Redman was slightly puzzled. "Then just tell the truth. You didn't know the camera was the same one. It never occurred to you. You were acting under instruction from Covet to supply Buckrack with what he demanded. You're not responsible for what he subsequently did with it. Let the police work it out from there."

"But I already lied to the CIA guy! I said I knew who Buckrack was when first shown his photo, but at the follow-up meeting I stonewalled and told them nothing. What if Nesbit knows that? If I bring Buckrack into it, it looks like I've been covering something up."

"Well," Redman shrugged, "you have. But so what? The CIA guy had no jurisdiction. You weren't obliged to tell him anything about an employee. He wasn't investigating the crime, only asking about Buckrack. He ambushed you."

"But, but – if this murder enquiry takes on a new life then we are right back in the shit again! We just clambered out of it. Imagine the press coverage. And, and – what will the Vice Chancellor think? He'll blame it on me."

"Then," said Redman, "best to tell him in advance. Not that blaming you would be wide of the mark, you understand."

Asterisk's hearing, or his attention, or both, were by now fading in and out. At his own evocation of McNamara's office, his distress seemed to reach its highest peak. "Oh God! Nesbit will find the invoices for the listening devices! He'll know they were ordered with my knowledge. He'll know they exist and that our denial of them was all a bluff. If that gets into the public domain, I'm toast. But if it's discovered that the new Vice Chancellor also knew and concealed it, then – oh fuck, oh fuck." The last four words were mumbled in diminishing volume rather than exclaimed. He slumped back in his chair and wilted there, pupils beginning to dilate, gazing towards the window with more than a hint of the self-dramatising.

"Then I guess," Redman consoled, "it would be better if I am the one to speak to McNamara."

"No," responded Asterisk effortfully. "Or at least not now. Give me some time. As soon as he knows he is bound to intervene, or to confess publicly in order to wash his own hands, and either way I am the fall guy."

"The fall guy?" Redman guffawed. "You were an active conspirator in Odiumgate! You facilitated the bugging of our offices! You've been serially lying about the gravest of matters. We simply agreed to help you cover one thing up. That's not much for McNamara to confess to, that he didn't go public with your guilty secret."

Asterisk's facial expressions were now taking place in pronounced slow motion. His flesh felt heavy. He tried to summon his jowls to perform the minimal elastic gestures of regret, and failed. "Yes, I know, that's true, but it's been good for the University! Imagine the kerfuffle if it had come out on top of the murder, or the Trump affair. We are both aware of that. Give me a little more time to paper over the cracks. I'll think of something. A week."

Redman did not appear agreeable, but after a moment of unflinching facial blankness from Asterisk,[5] he blinked. "It's Monday. I will tell him by the end of the week. You have until then, but make sure you keep me posted on what you are doing. Recent history suggests that skulduggery is a field in which you have meagre talent."

Asterisk, now almost incapable of talking, waved a hand in benign gratitude. A moment later, Redman appeared to have faded and vanished from his room.

Redman sauntered, testicle-sensitive, across the quadrangle to the School of English, where he fell into the seat at his office desk and set to processing the flood of students' extenuating circumstances forms which, it now being exam time, had fallen to his lot. Students as a collective – seeking mitigation for their disastrous

[5] A sure sign, not that Asterisk was good at poker, but that, unknown to Redman, the Valium had now taken hold.

performance, or no performance at all, in examinations or coursework – appeared to have grasped that a hidden illness which could not objectively be diagnosed but could be deduced only from the sufferer's personal testimony, was a much surer bet than any sickness with traditional physical manifestations. The most egregious case piled one phantom DSM symptom upon another into a veritable psychiatric Everest whose summit enjoyed such thin air that it seemed unlikely that anyone could stand upon it and breathe:

since last year I have been formerly diagnosed with borderline personality dissorder, major depressive dissorder, post-traumatic stress dissorder, panick dissorder and currantly I have an active diagnosis of type-2 bipolar dissorder (tho I personally consider myself type-1 and hope 2 convince my doctors of this in the near future), on account of all these illneses, I have often found it difficult 2 concentrate on university work and worrying about not doing my work at times creates further anxiety illness as before I was diagnosed I know that I was hospitalised while at school for active suicidal ideation and mania, and that things could turn out very badly if I am not able as I was at school 2 convert academic failure into success on account of illnes, in fact last year, in my first year at Odium, I was again hospitalised after an actual suicide attempt caused by a manic episode (which I blame on the lack of a trigger warning before being forced 2 read Sylvia Plath's *The Bell Jar*, which I understandably did not finish, and in fact barely started, but also because my counsellor convinced me that I had been sexually assaulted when in fact I thought I had fallen in love), as for the 3 exams I missed, as well as all the others in which I did not do as well as I would of done in conditions of mental balance that I have not known since I was 11, I have recently been experiencing severe temptation 2 self-harm as well as suicidal ideation, I did seek advice from the city Mental Health Crysis Team, but the person there "sham-shamed" me (i.e. shamed me for suppozed shamming), an accusation which of course predictably redoubled my paranoyd symptoms and led 2 a mild drug overdoze (for which I was seperately hospitalised), more recently still I have had visual and hearing hallucinations, in one of the exams I sat, I saw no words on the page, only wriggling worms, for example, and the clock on the wall did not tick but made the sound of jackboots on tarmac, needles 2 say, such fantasies make my anxiety intense and worsen my depression, also the medication I take for anxiety attacks and mania sedates me, which makes me 2 sleepy 2 read, study, write or revise much, on most days impossible in fact, so on the grounds of these documented mental health problems (documents attached in 2 ring binders) I seek **MITIGATION** for all my module assessments this academic year as I successfully did last year on similar grounds

Zani Fabula

Redman did not even look into the grey binders. He ticked a vacant square on the form which read "Refer to EC Board for determination", and passed on, with a deep sigh, to the next student.

This one, however, proved to be a contrary revelation:

Throughout the academic year problems caused by British Sign Language interpreters failing to translate key concepts explained verbally by my lecturers have caused me some local difficulties. This was especially so in modules which covered French literary theory (there is, to give just one example, no BSL sign for "jouissance" or anything like it) though I was largely able to resolve the ambiguities of these failed translations by turning to the originals in written French, in which I am fluent.

However, for the first week of semester 2 my latest interpretation company forgot to book any support at all (see attached email dated 7 January). I have been trying to offset the weakness of communication and support in lectures by doing more individual study, but on 29 April I developed a sore throat which I assumed would clear up quickly. However, it gradually became more painful and I developed a fever which inhibited me in the revision for my remaining four examinations. My GP diagnosed it as acute tonsillitis on 9 May and I was prescribed a course of antibiotics. (Please see attached GP letter dated 9 May.)

In fact, it turned out to be glandular fever, which worsened as the exam period went on, and resulted in serious pains in the throat and stomach area during my penultimate exam ("Metafiction and Metacriticism Part 1"). I went to the doctor's immediately afterwards and was referred almost instantly to A&E. I was hospitalised that evening with glandular fever and liver tenderness (my pain during the exam in fact originated in the liver rather than the stomach) and treated with a course of stronger antibiotics. I therefore perforce missed the final examination ("Early Eighteenth Century Satire") the following day. I was kept in for two nights and discharged on 17 May. (Please see attached letter from the hospital.)

Although I have been quite severely ill throughout the examination period, I feel I honestly did my best in the examinations I sat, and am confident that I have passed them all. I therefore seek only the opportunity to sit my last exam for the first time during the August resit period, if necessary, and if possible. It represents 50% of the module mark.

Alice Dean

Christ, thought Redman, tears almost pricking his eyes in cosmic surprise: a genuine case, accompanied with such a monstrously modest request, when so much more could have been made of it. He glanced at the supporting documentation, three single sheets of terse, unsentimental *dicta*: tonsillitis, glandular fever, swollen liver, antibiotics, failure of sign language interpretation agency to reserve a translator, student bodily incapacitated. Solid medical fact, undisputed institutional failure, unquestionable corporeal collapse of student, whose revival was then indubitably effected with proper hard drugs.

And so he pulled his keyboard towards him to write Alice Dean an email to say that she could take a first sit of the exam at the beginning of September. Before doing so, he pushed the paper form aside without marking it, and checked the student's run of provisional marks for her six modules: 86, 74, 72, 78, 38 (the coursework component of the module for whose other half, the exam, she had been absent) and 94 (a French Language option, the student having been exempted from oral examinations on grounds of disability). Everything was first class, much of it extremely so. No one with marks like that even required mitigation. It was already a first-class degree profile. Alice was an academic in the making if ever he had seen one, and probably a better one than him; indeed, a Dean already.

Shaking his head in sustained private bewilderment, but with a small yet positive sensation effervescing at the core of him, like someone who has plunged accidentally into a cold dank pond only hearteningly to witness a single large diamond gleaming warmly upon its sedimented vegetable bed, he started tapping the keys.

Chapter Three

McNamara's favourite joke about the Deputy Registrar, Elfyn Dethbridge, presupposed his being shipwrecked alone on a desert island. Rescued many years later, the joke ran, Dethbridge proudly showed his rescuers two separate wooden structures he had erected with his own hands in the jungle. When asked what their purpose was, Dethbridge replied in his broad Welsh accent, "Well, that one's the chapel I go to, and that one's the chapel I don't go to."

There was something which Dethbridge had moral reservations about erecting with his own hands, however, and that was his penis, for he belonged to a dwindling, pathetic and, in the twenty-first century, wholly superannuated subculture: he was a guilty gay.[6]

---

[6] One is tempted to draw adverse attention to the unremitting and unfashionable homophobia of C(l)ockman's narration. It rears up in every volume of the trilogy, centred on Avril Poon in volume one, dispersed among Dethbridge, Spooner and the two Islamic characters who figuratively read from the Queeran rather than the Quran in volume two, and is refocused through the lens of Dethbridge in this volume *passim*, but one should refuse to take umbrage. After all, apart from the likely postmodernist irony which may be adduced in

He had watched with incredulity and horror, after twenty-eight sexually mature yet disappointing years of a generally unfulfilled forty-year old life, as the LGBT revolution swept miraculously across campus between the end of one academic year and the beginning of the next, like the shockwave from a silent bomb, raising like associated monoliths four letters symbolising some instant USSR-type revolution in the sexuality sphere, reducing all the complex, conflicted history of his own gay conscience, his immense agon, his *Elfyn in Fairyland*, to four characters which, as far as he could tell, stood for four things which had hardly anything in common. In his private life, Elfyn avoided Ls and Bs like a bad cold and the 'flu respectively, and most certainly ran from Ts like the plague. He had perforce a little more to do with Gs, out of a certain compelling bodily necessity which assailed him every so often, but he was generally wise enough to take excursions far from Odium in order to indulge this nefarious habit, putting much wander into his lust. He attended many weekend events (and often took longer, physically strenuous vacations) in Brighton, and dreamed of being Registrar of one of the universities there.

He was unaware that many heterosexual male students shared his disappointment at the trending LGBT monopoly being enforced in discourse on sexual

---

defence of this irreverent gay-bashing, we can hardly claim that heterosexuality comes away from these fictions unmolested. Rather, it would appear that an understandable kind of Swiftian disgust at *all* sexual conduct and motivations is being relentlessly exercised. This anti-copulation motif should commend itself to asexual readers, such as the present commentator, who are too little catered for by literature in general.

matters among modern western youth, to the extent that to admit to being heterosexual or to live out the consequences of such an outmoded sexuality was now (they thought) seen by the young as a kind of death-in-life or, at least, a dreadful bore. But he was doubly appalled when (as he believed) these uncomplicated heterosexuals cleverly crafted two letters onto the end of the loathed abbreviation (LGBT + IQ) in order to enhance their own sexual credibility as "intersex" or "questioning", vague terms which were obviously invented in order to maximise their opportunities in being made to feel welcome in the bedrooms of dimwitted female undergraduates, who might in such loci then answer their many questions by allowing sex to pass between them.

Elfyn's fortunes in vagina-free penisandbumland were not enhanced by a pustular complexion, prematurely greying and thinning hair, more-than-incipient flabbiness of the gut, an awkward demeanour in social situations and, of course, his irremediable Welshness. But he had discovered over the years that physical abjection served him well. Men of his type of less-than-average personal attractiveness could more often than not compensate for their mediocrity if they presented a sexually servile aspect to their conquering knight with his super-extended lance. In just the last few days, indeed, he had been congratulating himself on his recent supine congress in an unusually local hotel with a significantly younger man from Spain who had, without money having to change hands for phallic favours to be dispensed, scorched Elfyn's lips with the frictional effects of his shuttling dude piston, and also turned his bowels into a split bag of mince by playing the aforementioned organ to diapason intensity inside the Cymric ring of his clutching anus, a virtuosity which had elicited loud Welsh solo vocal accompaniment.

That is, he congratulated himself on the encounter until the photographs and video (and almost simultaneously, the guilt) arrived in the mail. In a form which preserved them for posterity,[7] Elfyn did not find the ululations forced out of his mouth by a stiff yoghurt gun being forced into his anus quite so euphonous as he had imagined them at the time. He thought he had cried aloud with cinematic fervour; on the video, by contrast, it appeared to be a mixture of repeated grunts and squeaks, too porcine for personal dignity. Moving pictures of his rear attendant chasing him up Bournville Boulevard were unflattering to watch, but one particular still photograph on the USB stick, cropped and zoomed, showed something thick and sinewy like the end of a gym rope disappearing into his mouth to such a depth that his nostrils flared in the search for air and his eyes were crossed on account of maximised headspace pressure or nascent hypoxia. Visually, at least, it did not present the appearance of a dignified or even pleasurable pursuit. In fact, Dethbridge had enjoyed this free movement of the Spanish people so much that he had been forced to nurse some post-coital regrets at having voted for Brexit.

His mobile phone rang soon after he received the indecent package, the caller's number withheld. He

---

[7] It seems more probable that Dethbridge was concerned with a less remote possibility than "posterity" suggests, unless that word's relation to "posterior" is consciously kept in mind: he did not want film of him receiving a load up his rear tube to be uploaded to YouTube.

answered somewhat absent-mindedly, his reactions still hobbled by the shock in that morning's post, and heard what sounded like an American voice say, "My, what a big mouth you have."

Dethbridge felt his eyes widen involuntarily and a certain chill creep up the back of his neck. "Who is this?"

"Oh," said the voice, American, now most definitely American. "I'm a friend of Tomás. You remember Tomás, the guy I paid to pick you up and fuck you a few nights ago after I'd installed the camera, with his consent, in the ceiling corner of his hotel room? Amazingly high resolution, these modern mini-cameras, as you can see. And Tomás wasn't cheap, so I am expecting more than a little gratitude for my investment in your pleasure."

"Gratitude?" Dethbridge echoed hoarsely, incredulous and scared. "But, but, but you are trying to blackmail me, obviously. This video, these photographs! It won't work if you are trying to out me. My colleagues already know I am gay."

The person on the other end of the call did not laugh, but made a short sound of satisfaction which felt, to Dethbridge, that it must be accompanied by at least a smile. "Oh no, I'm not trying to do that. There is, of course, a difference between people knowing about your lifestyle in the abstract and getting to see it in all its real cock-gagging glory with you writhing naked beneath a stiff Iberian prong, and one almost half your age, incidentally. But no, it is not my intention to publicise the vigorous packing of your fudge. I am hoping that will not be necessary. All I really wanted to do was grab your attention so that you listen to me well."

At the amazing two sentences which followed, Elfyn Dethbridge – ever one to be seduced by dramatic prospects offered by individuals he sensed to be excitingly bolder than he was – pricked up his ears.

"I can help you become the next Registrar of the University of Odium," said the voice. "This will almost certainly happen if you follow my instructions."

A couple of hours later, McNamara, in his sumptuous office, was listening respectfully to the Head of the School of Earth Sciences, Professor Adrian Plumb. Plumb was more eccentric than McNamara remembered from having met him a couple of times in the previous decades. He was due to retire at the end of this academic year, and what McNamara recalled of the man's notable, earlier middle-aged vigour seemed to have withered away in his sixties. He was bald on top, had rheumy eyes, and displayed a slight but uncontrollable muscular tic on the right side of a mottled face centred on a now-swollen red nose. Gone was the smart suit he was always wont to sport on his then athletic, mid-forties body. He was now corpulent, wearing ill-fitting jeans and a grubby thin sweater, its sleeve-ends visibly abraded, the surface of it pock-marked with tiny pills of extruded, tangled fibres. McNamara wondered silently what had happened to diminish the man's physical condition (forgetting that his own outward appearance had only recently been effortfully raised from something rather worse than it), and thought, probably the usual: drink, divorce, the sedentary life, and creeping impotence.

Plumb had for a long time enjoyed considerable local celebrity on campus because he had, thirty years before, written a detailed geological history of the unusual promontory on which the University of Odium had been constructed, a tome which had proved revolutionary (or so it was bruited, by Plumb) in the teaching of his subject to first-year undergraduates. In their first semester of study these students now did not need to go on expensive, short-lived field trips to distant sites of earthly note, but instead to buy his thus ever-in-print expensive volume, by means of which they were taught to understand geology by reading the evidence of the immediate environment they saw daily all around them in the University grounds. Plumb's research for the book had also made him a terrific (if limited) raconteur in a way earth scientists seldom are: as long as you met him on campus and nowhere else, he could tell you virtually anything about the specific square metre of clay or silt or bog on which you were standing, or the building you were sitting in, when it went up, and the kind of foundations upon which it relied to remain fixed in the soil. He was, in this rather confined sense, monarch of all he surveyed, and his right there was none to dispute.

"I mean the caves directly under this building, the ones at the very bottom of the rock," Plumb was explaining in a slightly excited, nervous, high-pitched, etiolated chatter. "You know, you go down the concrete steps on the west side of this building to the parkland path, turn left and walk along the trail for a hundred metres or so, and they abut the shore of the lake, or rather the artificially created pond we call the lake. There are three large cavities in the rock, at least twenty feet high and thirty feet across, leading into the rockface, below the overhang."

"I know them," McNamara said. "But they are not in our purview. They're on the far side of the fence separating the park from the University. It's city council land."

"And that's the problem! No one at the city council planning department will take me seriously! This building was built on this rock ninety years ago, but we don't control the cliff wall on the park side, have never needed to. After all, it's just a cliff wall, isn't it? But this entire crag, whose sheer side it is, is ultimately nothing but soft limestone. And it's giving way! In the first cave, as you come along the path from here, there's now an enormous four-foot-wide fracture on the floor inside, extending inwards from the last fifteen feet of the cave and tapering laterally, getting wider as it recedes, possibly under and beyond its back wall too, deep into the structure. I don't know when it first developed, but it wasn't there a year ago. And the other two caves have now developed similar fault lines in their interiors. There's no saying when they will give. If these cracks are originating beneath the base of the rock, we're literally standing on shaky ground."[8]

[8] See, obviously, Matthew 7, 24-7: "Therefore whosoever heareth these sayings of mine, and doeth them, I will liken him unto a wise man, which built his house upon a rock: And the rain descended, and the floods came, and the winds blew, and beat upon that house; and it fell not: for it was founded upon a rock. And every one that heareth these sayings of mine, and doeth them not, shall be likened unto a foolish man, which built his house upon the sand. And the rain descended, and the floods came, and the winds blew, and beat upon that house; and it fell: and great was the fall of it." And so, I must issue a spoiler alert (I here speculate). While not as fully realised as their ancestral literary correspondents at Marabar, one intuits that the paragraphs introducing these hitherto unmentioned caves appear to constitute a passage to end things. I cannot be alone in predicting that they are an obviously contrived premise, slotted in here excrescently in order to forestall later accusations of irresponsible reliance on a *deus ex machina*, for the sudden cessation of odiousness

Though they seemed to have been scooped into the yielding escarpment by three giant spoons, the caves had been naturally formed by ancient subsidence, Plumb specified (not failing to specify that the cause was not erosion, as no river had ever flowed in the seeming valley below): this is what made him suspect that collapse was possible at any time. McNamara let him prattle on, screening out most of his technical jabber, looking with feigned attentiveness as Plumb pulled out drawings, photographs and a contour map from a box file he had placed self-importantly on the desk. He was privately more concerned with the pain in his back, which seemed to be flaring up once more.

The gaping cave mouths were magnets even to the least curious, especially passing youth, he reflected while half-listening to Plumb. The first time he had encountered them himself, many years ago, he had not been able to resist the temptation to enter and explore. They were not considered dangerous, as they penetrated to a depth of perhaps only forty or fifty feet. And he knew that none of them had had any pits in their floors to catch the unwary, as Plumb was now saying one or all of them did. They had thus become a haunt of underage drinkers, drug users and roomless lovers. The

---

promised in the novel's title. Just as the plot chaos will predictably arrive at an irresolvable complexity, expect this suddenly invented gash in the crust of things to erupt yet further so that the now Elsinore-like summit on which the University is arrayed is swallowed entire into the depthless chasms of the earth. Hence the novel's incongruous geological prologue, I now also suspect. This is the sort of thing that has to be made to happen when you attempt to represent the complexities of real academic life by means of the simplicities of thrillerdom.

last time McNamara had gone there, which he had to admit to Plumb was a good few years ago, there was graffiti on the walls at each cave entrance, broken bottles, condoms, and even the odd discarded syringe.

He eventually despatched Plumb with a promise to contact the city council above the lowly level of its planning department. The additional assurance that he would escalate the issue all the way to dizzy mayoral heights if necessary (insincere because the Vice Chancellor had already decided that Plumb was immeasurably more cracked than the cave floors over which he expressed such exaggerated concern) meant that the geologist left with a tight little smile on his face, exhibiting a slightly masonic smugness he had not often enjoyed but did perennially desire, appearing to be gratified by the fleeting arseprint he had left on the seat of power.[9]

McNamara sat in silence for a few moments, decidedly enjoying a brief fantasy, which had recurred

[9] Indeed, Plumb dreamed that night of being an astronaut atop a gargantuan meteorite falling towards Earth's surface with what would be unignorable consequences, woke in an extremely enlivened mood, went out for a bracing five kilometre morning run which Redman would have considered a breeze, but felt the beginnings of pains in his chest upon his panting return. At his funeral ten days later his estranged wife (for McNamara had almost been right about that: divorce proceedings had already been initiated) felt extremely pleased, beneath her wholly simulated grief, that she – not he – would receive a handsome sum from his pension fund upon his convenient death in service, as well as not have to continue all the legal bother she had recently set in train in order to rid herself of him. McNamara too was thankful, for it meant that he need never honour his promise to pursue the matter of the putatively crumbling caves Plumb foresaw as a threat to the University's existence.

ever since he had assumed his novel position and which he liked to indulge in brief moments of respite, of being a beleaguered captain of industry with whom many now sought an audience. The quiet hiatus was ended by the sound of his desk phone. It was his newly appointed, quiet, efficient Chinese personal assistant, Meifeng, whom he had personally rescued from the redundancy he had almost brought upon her in Chongqing, an act of patronage for which she was insanely grateful and fantastically loyal, and in respect of which he was endlessly self-congratulatory.

"Vice Chancellor," she said crisply, "we have lunch in five minutes with the group visiting from Taiwan. But there is a member of staff on the phone who is asking to see you urgently. Shall I schedule an appointment for later this afternoon?"

McNamara groaned operatically, putting a hand to his troubled brow. "Who is it?" he asked irritably.

The reply came, again with Meifeng's ever-notable, entirely un-Chinese trademark, the flawlessly pronounced *r*: "Professor Buckrack."

"I'd describe it as skeletal," Drusilla Frost found herself saying on the phone twenty minutes afterwards, "as personnel records go."

"Skeletal, how?" McNamara asked in reply.

Drusilla flipped through the manila folder on her desk as she summarised its meagre contents, which she had just printed off from the University HR database. "There's a letter of appointment, standard. The salary is on the high end, I'd say. It's for one year only, research only, no teaching, ending in the coming September."

"Appointment to which department?"

"To your department, the Vice Chancellor's. That

48

and the wording and the short fixed term suggests it's what HR would call a consultancy research post."

"And what's that exactly?"

"As opposed to an academic research contract. The research output would be expected to be for internal consumption, in other words, not external publication."

There was a pause. Then McNamara asked, "So he's paid from my budget?"

"We'd have to check with payroll," said Drusilla, "but almost certainly, yes. It's not entirely unusual. What I mean is, it's not the only appointment HR ever made like that under Covet."

"What's the address?"

"Unusually," said Drusilla, with a first hint of the disreputable creeping into her voice, "a hotel in London."

"Who wrote the letter?"

"Well," Drusilla said, more languidly, "I don't know. They have templates which they adapt according to the circumstances. No one writes them as such. They are form letters."

"Who signed it?"

"The Head of Human Remains, of course. But then she signs all professorial letters of appointment."

"She signed it? Did she meet the guy?"

"I rather doubt it. You can imagine how many appointments we make in an academic year, especially before the start of the year. She probably just scrawls her signature on an immense pile, one after the other. I don't expect she meets these people, or certainly not most of them. And knowing Evan Covet as I did, it was probably an appointment he made directly."

"Okay, so Covet would have interviewed him?"

"There's no record of any formal interview. We have

a photocopy of his American passport, of course, a letter of employment clearance from immigration, but then they pretty much just do that if you let them see a valid passport, and a campus housing contract agreed after he arrived. He lives in one of those redbrick cottages on University Drive. You know, the ones opposite Carillion Hall. By the way, it's rent-free. That's in the letter."

"Is that also usual with such an appointment?"

"I'd say not. Free rent? We milk campus residents dry, when we can, usually."

"No application form?"

"No."

"Is there a job description?"

"No."

"A CV?"

"No."

"References?"

"No."

"So that's it?"

"Yes. Your own office may hold more records, though. But I found it odd too. And so I just thought to look at the data access record for the file. And what did I find? Weirdly, someone accessed that file this morning, about an hour or so before I did. Yet no one had done so in the entire six months previous."

Drusilla heard the sound of McNamara's fingernails drumming. "Who?" he finally asked.

"Can't say. Maybe someone in IT can tell you, if you ask. It was accessed at 11.33am."

After another short harrumphing pause, McNamara concluded, "Okay, can you send me the copies? Like, right now, send someone up with it?"

"Sure," she said. "I am seeing Dr Redman in a

moment, you know, to discuss the redundancies, as you asked. Is it okay if I ask him to drop it in to your secretaries if he is going back to the same building? It would save me finding one of my own staff to do it. Difficult, at lunchtime."

"Sure, but seal it and mark it confidential. I don't want anyone in this office opening it. And don't speak with HR yet either. They don't need to know."

"Naturally," Drusilla concluded, and hung up.

In the few minutes before Redman arrived, she reluctantly allowed her mind to circulate around the discomfort she now felt whenever Covet's name came up between her and McNamara. In the first few weeks of their relationship she had expended many words to her new-found paramour in bad-mouthing the dead Covet without ever, of course, alluding to the fact that her mouth had been carnally good to him many years before his death, when she was Deputy Director of Communications, eager for the promotion which had, after several months of concupiscence on his part and studied marital infidelity on hers, followed. Covet had then moved on (with a precipitate punctiliousness which he had portrayed as proper) to batten on greener and less potentially thistly pastures. Indeed, she came to feel that he had promoted her, not as an ample reward for the sexual bounty she had profligately made available on loan from her then sex-deductible spouse, Mr Macbeth,[10] but rather as interest on the principal

[10] Told you so. One notes, *en passant*, that almost exactly halfway through volume one of the trilogy the reader has already been urged to think of Covet himself as echoing the protagonist of the Scottish play.

when Covet efficiently returned it. Things had at first felt non-mercenary with McNamara, their genuine attachment being pursued in a spirit of mutual freedom and not with thought of gain on either side. They had even consciously disliked each other before, but their feelings had seemed to undergo some alchemical transformation as they had bonded in China, and that slight feeling of magic had persisted for a while between them. The fact was that she had never expected McNamara to step into Covet's death-vacated Vice Chancellorial shoes – who had? – and thus to find herself the serial occupant of two Vice Chancellorial beds. But this unlikely event had soured her spirit, as it had coincided with McNamara's sexual demands becoming unexpectedly more tyrannical. Once he had accepted the managerial position he seemed to wish her to assume all kinds of new erotic positions. Covet, to be sure, had been Emperor-like in his lecherousness, but his conceited smiles had always hinted at the promise of rich patronage to follow. McNamara, on the contrary, had begun to bang her like a whore he had already paid in advance. With the one, it was fornication with a view to improving her job prospects; with the other, it now felt like pornification in order to retain it.

The great complicators in these thoughts were Drusilla's lack of comforting delusions in her now appreciably post-menopausal phase of life. She tended not to harbour romantic fantasies, possessed no flatteringly deformed self-image, and was childlessly untroubled by maternal obligations. She knew, for example, that physically she was an overripe fruit, but calculated that, to older men especially, this did not render her inedible. Her mental abilities she subjected to the same ruthless, delusionless appraisal: no intellectual she, she knew that performative competence in dealing with the press and public on the glossy superficialities of institutional life demonstrated her intrinsic and acquired talents to their fullest extent. Sexually, she considered herself open-minded enough to adopt the traditional role, happy to be a pleaser without being pleased, aware that a deficit in her own bodily enjoyment was bonus-balanced, usually, by some compensatory benefit in another dimension of life. This was why she had never felt any reservation in welcoming older, uglier men into her bed, when they were status-enhancingly wealthy or powerful. Allowing them to feel they lorded it over her was what permitted her to lord it over others. She was skilled at identifying such men and deliberately flying into their regularly welcoming webs.

Younger men, she found herself instantly thinking once James Redman stepped into the room, were an entirely different matter. The impression he made was not the one she had expected. Redman, she was aware, had despised her for a long time – she, the ever-spinning weathervane in the constantly shifting corporate winds – although their cooperation during the tumultuous events of last term had perhaps softened the edge of his dislike. She had hoped this was so, not least because of the erstwhile (and presumably still existing) friendly association between him and McNamara. But what she had never seen in him before was *vulnerability*, as in his slightly off-balance demeanour today, the tinge of emotional flush in the cheek, the perceptible sign of dilation in the pupils and the hint of pheromones in the air around him. It did not take her very long to twig (recalling dimly something McNamara had privately said about the departing

Lorraine Quant) what was the likely, girlfriendless cause. Drusilla was something of a heat-seeking missile, and Redman was in heat. The younger man was unable to keep the rut out of his strut. His need for coition could not be hidden by volition. Within moments of his arrival, before the small talk was even over, Drusilla had concluded that right now this Redman would probably make do with even a scarlet woman. The other surprise she felt was that her curiosity at this intuition was not indifferent. It gave her a mental itch she felt an impulsive need to scratch.

"I presume," she said, "you got the attention you usually do when you pass through this office?"

Redman looked at her over the coffee she had given him, with what he thought was an innocent expression on his face, simultaneously wondering if she was mono- or multi-orgasmic. "I beg your pardon?" he said.

"Oh, the young things out there," Drusilla ingenuously smiled, gesturing through the wall, all the while picturing his topless form sliding down a similarly nudified female midriff, hovering over the navel with a hint of tongue (she was not yet sure if this was her own omphalos or someone else's). "It's no secret they consider you a looker."

This was an absolute lie. No one on Drusilla's staff trusted or liked her enough personally to divulge such perceptions to her, but she always found that a man's response to unverifiable but gratifying falsehoods revealed a great deal about his narcissism or his prurience, usually both.

"But there's no one in your outer office," Redman rejoined, confident that his expression was inscrutable, as in his mind's eye he casually reached across the desk and began to fondle Drusilla's pleasantly plump left

54

hooter with his right hand, pumping it like an old-fashioned motor horn, without complaint from her.

"Ah, it's lunchtime," she said smoothly. She had now decided that the carefully groomed pelvis which she imagined him kissing was definitely hers, and surprised and a little enchanted to envisage a full head of male hair down there in that spot, where she normally saw only the monkishly bald or balding. "Otherwise I'm sure you would have been the object of many coy smiles and sidelong looks. It must be all that exercise you do."

Redman coughed. He was already visualising three of her blouse buttons undone and his fingers confidently stroking her revealed cleavage. Reality impinged for a moment as he fancied he glimpsed a push-up bra whose purpose could only be dis-hearteningly anti-gravitational, but he dismissed this impediment to his wholly subjective pleasure deftly, as in his fantasy he arose, unzipped, and yearningly pulled out his banana and coconuts, and presented them to her invitingly on the desktop with a resounding scrotum-slap.[11] "Shall we talk about the redundancies?"

Drusilla readily agreed, while privately speculating, with a disguised but unforeseen internal frisson, that a younger fitter bull like Redman might even make her something she had always wanted to be: orgasmic.

Elfyn Dethbridge had been contemplating all day something even more enticing, he was perplexed to discover, than male sexual organs. Ever since his blackmailer had that morning introduced the prospect

---

[11] The important function Redman performs in this novel is, quite literally, to be a load of balls.

of the Registrarship of the University of Odium to his distressed wits, he had been like a cat who suddenly notices a bright shining light on the floor. He had quite put aside the extortionate circumstances in which the hope had been planted. Now he wished simply to pounce, and secure it as a reality.

"That's all there is?" rasped his consternated American blackmailer down the phone. "An appointment letter, a passport photocopy, an immigration clearance, and a housing contract? Have you left anything out? Are you fucking with me?"

"No, of course not," said Dethbridge, who was already feeling, without knowing it, something of the peculiar romance of Stockholm syndrome. "Why would I do that? But how does this help me become the next Registrar of the University of Odium?"

"It doesn't," came the reply. "Not on its own. This doesn't get you very far. There are a few more simple steps you'll need to take to unseat Asterisk."

Dethbridge started a little in his soul, as the cat does when the light on which it leaps just as quickly vanishes. "Who is this Buckrack guy anyway? Why did you want his employment info?"

"Never mind that," was the blunt response. "I need you to tell Asterisk. Send him an email after close of business today saying that Buckrack is back in town. Then report to me on any reaction tomorrow morning. I'll call you again later this evening with further instructions."

Dethbridge's inner feline suddenly spotted the light aglow elsewhere on the carpet, and was excited that it had not disappeared altogether. Nonetheless, he allowed this peremptorily issued order to whirr gently through his pleasingly abused cat-mind. "But how would I know that?"

"Easy," said the cold-blooded voice. "Tell him Buckrack called you up and asked you to pass on the message."

Chapter Four

McNamara had (wisely, he thought) deflected Buck-rack's telephone request for a meeting. He told Meifeng to take Buckrack's number and say she would call him back. He wanted to be better prepared and not taken by surprise. With the little further information he had gleaned from Drusilla he decided to ponder the matter throughout the rest of the day's activities.

The visit of the Taiwanese delegation – members of the board of their scholarship awards body for post-graduate research in the arts – was not McNamara's idea. It had been organised by Professor Alexander Whipsaw, the Head of American and Pacific Rim Studies (a position which dictated that its incumbent was popularly called, unknown to Whipsaw, "Chief Rimmer"). But as it was something the University could not have entertained while it was hand-in-glove with the Chinese government, McNamara now welcomed it, and had decided to push the boat out in order to woo the delegates into parting with some of the three million U.S. dollars they controlled.

Having met the delegates formally at a brief lunch in his oak-panelled private dining room, he retired to his office while Whipsaw rimmed them on a conducted tour around the campus to make whistle-stop visits to the departments that concerned them. Everyone, including most of the heads of those departments, would convene again for a grand, gold-prospecting, tongue-convoluting dinner in the evening. Chivers had come from the Vice Chancellorial house to organise the numberless flunkies, ensuring that they whizzed around the dining room all afternoon.

Redman delivered the confidential data from Drusilla to Meifeng a while later. When she brought it to him, McNamara saw a post-it note on the flap which read, "Too busy to drop in, but met with D. and will talk to you soon. Am working on the details today. James."

He scolded himself at having largely ignored Buckrack and all the historical drama associated with him since becoming Vice Chancellor. Scrutiny of the few documents inside the envelope told him no more about the man than he had already learned verbally from Drusilla. He called Meifeng back into his office and asked her to look in the departmental files for any further information on Professor Buckrack. She returned within fifteen minutes and told him she could find nothing.

The remainder of his work day passed without unexpected event. Mostly he had Buckrack at the back of his mind, but the thoughts went nowhere, merely whirling around and around in an inconclusive loop. He searched for him on the internet and found nothing.

The ache in his back had not gone away. It was an unignorable button of misery just below his rear ribs. He took two codeine tablets to dull it.

Meifeng popped in and out at intervals, in her efficient way, bringing documents for signature, materials to read, proposals for meetings. Each time she did so she never failed to give him a smile which radiated gratitude and authenticity. The last couple of times she did so he found himself admiring her pointy breasts under her neatly ironed pink blouse.

At 5.15pm, with everyone else in the outer office gone, he invited her back in.

"Sit with me and have a drink before we go to the dinner," he said. He had come to enjoy this benefit of his office, the unquestioned ability to frame requests as imperatives. It made him feel like the demanding Richard Burton in *Where Eagles Dare*. He liked the way it made some people seem uneasy. It was a clever method of ascertaining how comfortable they were with him. And Meifeng (just like the women cast in *Where Eagles Dare* for this seemingly same sole purpose) looked genuinely pleased, as if being permitted a rare privilege. "This is what is called an ... apéritif?"

"Yes," he said. "Dry rather than sweet, usually. Mine's a gin and vermouth. What can I give you? The same? Or white wine?"

She deliberated briefly, and smiled again. "I would like to try what you are having."

"Two Martinis it is." He began to scoop ice cubes from a concealed fridge into two funneled glasses, and completed the concoctions at a similarly hidden liquor cabinet. "President Franklin D. Roosevelt did this every day for an hour with his staff around this time. There was one rule: no one present could talk about work. So let's follow his rule."

Actually, he wanted the slightly improper feeling of seeming intimacy with a woman whom he had at a disadvantage, moreover one who accepted the inequality between them, who regarded him with nothing but a sense of appreciative indebtedness. He felt unperturbed, therefore, at his desire to watch her sitting on his couch in a more reclining pose than usual, her stockinged legs angled and her breasts jutting towards him conically.

They talked, mostly about her. Meifeng seemed to acknowledge entirely his right to ask her about her family, how she was settling in Britain, her past as a student in St Andrews and Durham, how she spent her free time, and so on, without seeming to assume that she could ask similar questions in reply. She seemed, indeed, delighted by the attention. She accepted a second drink with alacrity, apparently amazed that he was prepared to spend any personal time with her.

McNamara continued to enjoy looking at her legs, and her breasts, and her jet-black hair, and her eyes, and her mouth. And she smelled good too.

At 6pm they bestirred themselves and walked along the corridor to the pre-dinner drinks reception. At the dinner itself, with considerable experience of these formal events under his belt, McNamara had himself buffered from the obsequies of the Taiwanese by ensuring that he had Meifeng on his right (for translation needs as required but, he noted, with additionally pleasurable benefits of the scented kind) and Whipsaw on his left, with the English-speaking head of the Taiwanese delegation, Professor Lin, opposite him, flanked by two other Odium heads of department.

The Taiwanese proved (contrary to McNamara's experience of the Chinese) to be unexpectedly relaxed and exponentially bibulous. In the lull between the main course and dessert, with much drink already having been taken by all, several of the delegates and their hosts were actually on their feet singing Beatles' songs, acapella, to tables full of smiles. It was proving to be a successful event. In the middle of "Yesterday" Professor Lin announced that he liked scotch. McNamara instantly called Chivers over and instructed him to bring them a bottle of eighteen-year-old Inchmurrin. It was liberally passed around. Twenty minutes later, seeing the popular demand, he asked for another.

Even though he was approaching full-on (real-life, not in character) Richard Burton now, he turned to Meifeng with the idea of impersonating someone even more famous, and said, "Let's do the old JFK and Jackie thing." After he had explained what this meant, they slowly toured the table like the presidential couple, shaking hands with everyone and spending a few moments exchanging pleasantries with each Taiwanese individual. They returned to their seats and McNamara beamingly drank more whisky, occasionally inclining to whisper confidentially into Meifeng's ear. As he was close to finishing his third or fourth large tumblerful, he realised with a sudden drunken intensity that he had forgotten entirely about Buckrack. An impulse to address this long-lingering problem assailed him. He looked at his watch. It was not yet 9pm.

"Meifeng," he said, "I need to borrow you for a moment." She looked surprised, in the way that a piece of property might raise a baffled eyebrow (if a piece of property possessed eyebrows) when its owner asked to borrow it, and followed him closely and obediently out of the room. They walked side-by-side along the corridor to the Vice Chancellor's suite of offices. McNamara had only a few minutes before been fantasising about doing just this in order to take Meifeng there and lay hands proprietorially upon her slim, cuspate body, but was now scolding himself inwardly at having entertained an indecent reverie for several hours about this mere underling and her sheer underthings. Nonetheless, he still stole sidelong covetous glances at her shuttling stockinged legs, her wiggling rear end and her bountifully bobbing bicameral bosomy bulges.

"So funny," Meifeng remarked. "I have never met so many Taiwanese people together in one place. I liked them."

"Ah, yes," said McNamara, "of course, the three tees one is told never to mention in China: Taiwan, Tibet, Titshandlingmen Square..."

They had reached the door of the outer office. Meifeng had her key in the door and hand on the knob. She looked at him quizzically. Was it his boozy imagination, or had she just bodaciously boosted bra-braced Beijing-bred boobies towards him?[12]

He smiled playfully and, to cover his fatigue-fuelled Freudian faux pas, improvised. "Forgive me, it's a vulgar old man's joke."

She seemed, thankfully, unoffended. He blustered his way into her office and asked her to call Buckrack and tell him that he was too busy to meet with him the next day, but that, as it was urgent, he should come to the Vice Chancellor's house that night at ten o'clock.

Meifeng did as she was told. Buckrack did not answer her call. She left a voicemail.

They went back to the winding-down dinner and McNamara, pleading graciously the onerous duties of a British university Vice Chancellor, made his exit. He would leave the Taiwanese in the capable hands of Meifeng, thinking as he said so that he would have

---

[12] The answer is no: Meifeng was born and raised in Nanjing.

preferred to have had her left in his own incapable hands.

It was still light as he went out of the rear entrance of the Trump building, dusky, overwarm. He shambled up the hill in his unventilated, now tight-seeming three-piece suit, sweaty from the drink and his lustful orientation, pissant-concupiscent, thinking not of the lack of an air conditioner in the dining room but the absence of Meifeng's hair conditioner in his olfactory bulb, in the growing bad mood which impossible-to-satisfy sexual urges inevitably create when cocktailed with too much whisky. But at least, he reflected, the plentiful alcohol seemed to have kept at bay the inveterate throbbing in his back.

He was thankful in his knowledge that the house would be empty. Drusilla was visiting her ailing mother in her care home in London overnight and would not return until tomorrow afternoon; Chivers had been given the next morning off on account of his having done a back shift at the dinner. The prospect of a late-morning lie-in was gratifying: he had, in fact, no appointments at all the following forenoon. But the wish at last to encounter Buckrack, to confront him if necessary, was now an intoxicating imperative he lacked the judiciousness to delay.

He got out of his suit and had a quick shower, changed into comfortable clothes, went downstairs and treated himself to another large scotch. It was 9.40pm. It was dark now. Nothing happened at 10 o'clock except the pouring of another whisky. No one arrived. Perhaps Buckrack had not listened to the voicemail?

It was not for another quarter hour, as he was contemplating yet more stiff drinks, that the doorbell rang.

*

Redman was still sitting in his narrow office. It was dingy and confining, so dark indeed that even on a bright early summer day like this one he had to turn the main light on at 5.30pm. Despite the fact that it was on the ground floor at the rear of the building facing a blank, peeling grey wall, and had bars on the windows to deter burglars, it was nonetheless a room a Party apparatchik on the level above the execution chambers in the Lubyanka would have been jealous to occupy.

As McNamara sat with his Martini on his grey office Davenport, his penis mildly tumefied by his surreptitious eyeing of Meifeng's beshirted but discernibly acuminate chesticles, Redman had been periodically adjusting the hang of his hyper-ballic scrotum as it balanced on the edge of his swivel chair. He continued to toil, sometimes standing to ease his distressed cullions, through the entire period of the Taiwanese-honouring banquet taking place in another wing of the building, above a desk littered with spreadsheets and budget reports and personnel lists, an angled reading lamp washing their printed data in an extra-stark white light. He had a prized fountain pen which he used on special occasions, and could not think how it could be more fittingly deployed than in its sharp tungsten nib helping bureaucratically to slit the throats of known enemies and identifiable wasters and to score other dead wood which choked the congested and stagnating industrial canal of the University of Odium.

Time was short. The general letter announcing the redundancy procedure would go out to all staff the following day, and collective hysteria and paranoia could therefore be expected instantly the following afternoon. Recommendations for redundancy would be sought from heads of departments, but in reality this is not how human decimation works in a twenty-first century British university. Those to be executed would be chosen in advance by a trusted functionary like himself, and his reward would be not only that his own skin was saved, but that he got to enjoy the power over profess-ional life and death that he now wielded on paper, a pleasure whose psychological importance has been little studied but is much understood by those who partake of it.

Before him he had up-to-date information on departmental incomes and expenditure as well as dreadful forecasts for the same for the coming academic year, listings of individuals' salaries and research monies they each had generated, and estimates of the cost of making individuals redundant based on their years of service. His official remit was almost entirely arithmetical: he was to target deficit-budget departments, theoretically to rebalance their budgets until they were prospectively ten percent in the black by recommending individual redundancies (because this surplus would in a short time pay for the anticipated redundancy costs), and forward this list to McNamara, who would then instruct the Head of HR to organise show trials for the pre-condemned individuals and arrange simultaneously for rifles to be loaded (in the form of prepared dismissal letters) for the firing squads which would follow on a date already specified at the end of June, namely the earliest date redundancy law permitted, so that the decks would be cleared and the blood hosed away before the beginning of the new academic year in late September.

But Redman was not by nature inclined to arithmet-ical procedures: he was more geographically minded, and decided to slay his closest enemies first. He walked (in his mind) coolly down the corridor and lacerated the jugular of his own Quisling Head of Department, Bernard Matthews, and that of the dentally challenged Glaswegian Trotskyite troll, Donald Dooley. Next he sought out Sergei Krokoff, engaged him in seemingly innocent conversation, but stuck a rag in his mouth as soon as he started ejaculating malapropistic sentences, so that the Ukrainian soon choked on his own bad English as it gathered in his windpipe, eventually leading to a greater-than-usual laryngeal prominence which, as Redman turned his back and left the room, blew a hole in the front of Krokoff's neck and sent a gelatinous spray of ill-chosen lexis onto the wall. He proceeded upstairs and summarily put to death Professor Gallstone and (sweet to witness her dark artery ripping) Associate Professor Poon. He crossed to the south side of the building and stalked the corridor in search of Reinhardt McGuile, the smooth-talking saurian Chair of Romance Languages; but McGuile's years of service were vast (almost three decades in post!) and the Department of Spanish, Portuguese and Latin American Studies was one of the few in the Arts to boast of a handsome financial surplus. It would be impolitic from a pecuniary point of view to dispose of him, no matter how much personal delight would be yielded by the offing of this learned goon who spoke five languages and of whom it was said that every time he farted an academic paper came out.

Redman eased his frustration by crossing to the Department of Russian and Slavonic Studies and leaving two carcasses in his wake. As he emerged from this scene of carnage he randomly encountered Dr Simeon Stylites, a ginger-headed balding bumbler who ran a pitiable postgraduate research outfit in Critical Theory, and cut him down gratuitously (Stylites was cheap to dispose of, with only five years' service), crushing his Adam's apple underfoot as he pulled out the blade. He took the elevator to the top floor and ran amok in Philosophy,[13] slipping on the resultant slime and viscera in the corridor as he subsequently traversed the same level to the French department, where he administered the *coup de grâce* to three (or four: he lost count) *autres*.

Gored to excitement in his imagination, he galloped down the stairs and left the building, sprinted down the hill, and went on a serial bloodletting in Art History, ending the barely interesting academic existence of, among others, Professor Miles Dudd, currently on recall from China, with minimal mercy and maximal pain. Exiting, he glanced across at the Department of History and noticed Professor Wilf Hindsight and his jolly Mexican wife, Dr Inés Retrospectiva, chatting amiably over cigarettes in the courtyard. He put an instant end to their smoking habit.

He jogged back up the hill (again, in his mind) to the Social Sciences building. There were three German

[13] One of the trio of here summarily noted liquidations in Philosophy was in fact savagely, synchronously ironic: at the very moment Dr Moynahan Pissant was struck down by Redman he was completing the "Working with Business" section of his personal university page with the following words: "I like working with business. I have with colleagues instituted a series of one-day training sessions for small companies in the Odium area centred on the theme of 'Making Ethical Decisions'. These draw upon existing philosophical research to help organisations make morally good hiring decisions and develop other principled employment practices."

leftists from the Department of Politics on his list. Ten minutes later, he was able to cross them off. When he emerged from the sliding doors of the building he noticed that his hands were trembling. He decided to take a brief break, returned to his office in the Trump building, and switched on his Italian coffee machine. He ate a couple of biscuits to replenish his sugar levels. He noted with medical interest that his vexatious arxidia now felt vastly more relaxed in their hot pouch than they had for several weeks. Fantasy slaughter was evidently therapeutic for them.

This had been merely the work of the afternoon hours. But Redman had by now no intention of stopping. He pressed on through the evening into the much less familiar territory of the science departments, where the research income was immeasurably more plentiful and deserving victims correspondingly much more tricky to identify. What was one to do, for instance, with someone like Professor Benjamin Fowle, who was in receipt of a grant of six million from the Engineering and Science Research Council to investigate the physical tolerances of various kinds of railway sleepers, but had not published one single-authored academic paper in five years, yet had had his name appended to over thirty articles written by members of his research team in the same period, the obvious bloody little sleeper that he was himself?[14]

---

[14] I have decided largely to allow the crazed academiphobia of this regularly cynical text to speak for itself, but I must confess that I am also (as a distinguished academic myself) rendered rather speechless by the virulence of the hatred towards workers in the intellectual sphere we can witness in this discourse. On the one hand, I consider most readers too enlightened to be swayed by the infantile wish-

Redman slashed his way through or appropriately avoided such thickets as they came at him, and by the wane of the long May day his one-man genocide in the University of Odium was at last at a satisfying end.

He looked at his watch. It was almost 10.30pm. How time flew when you were determining fates!

He picked up his phone and called McNamara. McNamara did not answer. Redman left a voicemail.

The message was: "Hi, Robert. James here. I've just finished the redundancy recommendations. I'll drop by on my way home and slip it through your letterbox. I know you tend to stay up late, so if you fancy a drink, I'd quite like one after all this work. So I'll ring your doorbell in hope. But if you are not there, or don't want to be disturbed, I'll talk to you tomorrow."

---

fulfilment impulses to which such satirical treatment of the academy panders (who, for example, would find even slightly credible the idea that men with considerable power and acting in accord with a grave public duty would expend so much libidinal energy in futile lust directed towards their female subordinates?). On the other, I know that there are ignoramuses and populist right-wing government ministers into whose laps it will readily be invited to dance. I vacillate, therefore, as to the degree to which I should intervene to correct this irresponsible text's obvious demerits and excesses in its parodic treatment of a serious and elevated institution. I state here that, after due ethical consideration, I reserve the right henceforth in these notes to set this frequently wayward novel on a proper moral course where I deem such action necessary. But one must not be too heavy-handed. I will only note for the moment (as a frequent railway traveller) that *someone* surely has to be in receipt of £6m (or perhaps more, who knows?) to investigate the physical tolerances of railway sleepers. If Professor Benjamin Fowle or his like has been given the boot (which is regrettably unclear from this passage), I worry for my personal safety while in transit, and so should you.

Chapter Five

McNamara at first wondered if Buckrack's failure to appear promptly at ten o'clock was deliberately intended to indicate a certain coolness on the American's part. But the breathless Buckrack's panting excuse (he had not listened to the voicemail from Meifeng until close to the appointed time and had rushed as fast as he could, briefcase in hand, up the hill from his campus house) suggested a satisfying sense of urgency. Good, McNamara thought: he really does need a meeting, he's apologetic, and I have the upper hand.

Buckrack was physically unimpressive. He was visibly around the same age as McNamara, and though somewhat less corpulent, his stomach in its white shirt nonetheless depended flaccidly over the waistband of his jeans. He was flushed and sweaty-faced from his exertions in the warm night, a little bug-eyed, even.

McNamara invited him in, let him sit on the couch, and asked him if he wanted a drink. Buckrack, seeing McNamara's already well drained bottle of single malt, elected to join him. Annoyingly, however, he asked for ice. McNamara went into the kitchen and got some, then returned and sat opposite, by now rather inebriated, yet feeling composed, determined to control his drunkenness by not saying very much but listening closely and attempting to be inscrutable. He said he was sorry that he had not been able to see Buckrack in the afternoon, and gestured at him invitingly to come to his business.

Buckrack took a breath and began. "We may have a problem. In fact, I think we do have a problem. It seems that, after what took place here in the university, you know, the Trump fiasco, that the American authorities have been asked to look into the death of the American student earlier in the year, the one your predecessor murdered. Of course they cannot investigate it directly or officially, although there are unofficial things they can do. In fact, I think you'll find that the case has already been re-opened and that the CID, a guy called Nesbit, spoke to the Registrar this morning."

McNamara paused. In some ways he thought his drunkenness was aiding his abilities in deciphering the man, slightly alienating him from his speech, enhancing his abilities to read between the lines. And McNamara was accustomed by now not to giving direct answers, or giving non-committal ones, or asking lots of questions of his own before he answered a single one himself. Most people who spoke to him wanted something, and he consequently was used to controlling the discourse he had with them.

"Let's come to the so-called problem in a moment," he said levelly. "You say that *we* have a problem. But right now, I am wondering who *we* even are. You know who I am, it's a matter of public record. But I hardly know who you are at all. I know that your salary is paid from my budget. I have your personnel record. It's extraordinarily thin as these things go. I know that you were hired last September as a research fellow. But I don't know what you've been doing. You don't seem even to have been here in the last six months. Your campus house appears to have been empty most of that time despite a free tenancy agreement. And, oddly for an academic, I can't find a single trace of you on the internet: no publications, no conference papers, no previous university posts. I'm frankly puzzled. Would you care to enlighten me?"

It was Buckrack's turn to hesitate. "There's a limited amount I can say," he prevaricated.

"I don't know why that should be," McNamara replied. "But try me with the limited amount."

"You know," said Buckrack after a time, "that it was me who told you about the bugs in the offices? That it was me who sent you those notes? That it was me who blew the gaff on Covet?"

"I did work that out eventually, yes," rejoined McNamara. "I knew you were on the committee looking into Jane Blake's complaint against Covet, and I worked backwards from there and surmised a little. Only a small number of people had access to those documents. But I can't figure out why. How did you even know there were bugs in our rooms?"

"Because," said Buckrack, "it was me who put them there."

McNamara let his eyes widen a little. "It was you who did that? Not Jane Blake?"

"It was one of the things Covet hired me to do. I wasn't really a research professor, and I have no academic background at all. That's why I wasn't attached to any academic department. It was just a cover. I was more of a ... consultant. I was paid to gather intelligence."

"You mean you were a spy, right?"

"If you like."

"Is that what you do?"

"I used to," said Buckrack. "I had a previous career in security services, let's say."

"Which one?"

"As I say, I can't tell you everything."

McNamara rubbed his nose and looked at Buckrack with narrowed eyes. "Alright, but why then tell us about the bugs? Why defeat your own purpose?"

"Look, that's irrelevant. It was good for you that I did, no? But if all of this is looked into again, it's going to be bad for all of us."

"For all of us? Why would it be bad for me? I didn't do anything."

"You knew. You lied. You covered it up."

"I didn't do anything. I denied nothing. No one asked me. I simply chose to remain silent about the fact that my privacy had been violated."

"Okay, sure, but if it all comes out now, that the bugs were real, that they really were put into private offices in this University by the ex-Vice Chancellor, think of the new public scandal you'll have to manage."

McNamara shrugged. "Then we'll manage it. It was a dead guy who did it. And you, of course, which is what I think you are more worried about. Your name will come up."

"Yes," Buckrack admitted. "And I can't let that happen."

"Tell me, why should it? You said they had re-opened the Jane Blake case. So they are looking again into her murder. What's that got to do with the bugs?"

Buckrack gave off the air of a man trying to be patient when he had very little time. "The CID spoke to Asterisk this morning. It was Asterisk who bought the bugs on his budget. Hardly anyone knows that. They were most likely asking him about the video camera, the one used to make the film of Covet and Blake having sex, but which wasn't found at the murder scene. They want to trace it, I am guessing."

"Wait a minute, wait a minute," McNamara interrupted. "Asterisk didn't only *know* about the bugs, he also *bought* them on his account?"

"Covet was covering his ass. If the bugs were ever found, he'd have blamed Asterisk. The paperwork would have been consistent with that claim. But we know they never were officially found. Everyone's forgotten about them. If Asterisk now tells the CID he bought the bugs on his account, he'll also tell them about me. And then you'll have to explain why this University hired an American spy to compromise its own staff."

"I see," said McNamara, still somewhat insouciant. "Yes, it'll be embarrassing, but not unmanageable."

Buckrack shook his head in exasperation. "You don't get it! I'm recently ex-CIA, okay! The story won't be that Covet hired a private snooper, it will be that a CIA guy – because no one will believe the 'ex' thing for a moment – planted bugs in an English university, that America is spying on its ally. Of course, this is total nonsense. Not even the Americans really know that this happened or that I was involved. Trump just thinks he's causing trouble for the University of Odium because you snubbed him publicly. He wants to teach you and the British government a lesson by dragging out the Jane Blake enquiry and casting aspersions against the British and whipping up patriotism at home while it goes on. The British know that's exactly what he's doing. They can't be too happy that this University put them in this fix. But they have to play along. Now, if the CID find out that a one-time American intelligence officer did the bugging, then the shit really hits the fan. It won't be CID on the case after that but MI5. I don't want to be in the centre of that tornado. Nor do you."

McNamara sat back and sighed. "Let me fix us another drink," he said.

He went into the kitchen once more for ice for Buckrack's scotch and returned, resuming his seat.

His phone suddenly rang. He looked at it briefly, saw that it was Redman, then let it go to voicemail.

"Explain to me," McNamara said, "because I am puzzled about it. This video camera, the one Jane Blake used, how come it's the one Asterisk bought? How did Jane Blake get hold of that?"

Buckrack bit his lip impatiently, then relented. "Let's say I became aware of Covet's exploitative relationship with Jane Blake. It was that that turned me against him, made me decide to destroy him rather than assist him. There are some moral lines I don't cross, even in my business. So I made contact with her and helped give her a way out of her predicament."

"A way out?" McNamara replied, with some heat. "She got herself killed!"

"That's true," Buckrack admitted. "But who could have predicted that?"

"It's the kind of shit that sometimes happens when you fuck about with people's private lives," McNamara said venomously.

Buckrack tilted his head in acknowledgment of a truth. "Unforeseen consequences. But as I was saying, in my line of work we have to make it a habit of getting to know exactly who we are dealing with. The same way I know, for example, about your holiday last Christmas in Amsterdam, your whore, your dope-smoking."

There was a long silence. McNamara stared at his interlocutor. The atmosphere in the room had entirely changed. He felt a throbbing in his temples and an ache beginning to creep into the back of his head.

"What are you talking about?" he finally said, quietly.

Buckrack grimaced. "I was there," he said.

He unsnapped his briefcase and put an envelope on the table between them, next to McNamara's tumbler of whisky. McNamara opened it slowly and shuffled out half a dozen photographs: him in the Amsterdam red light district, him hand in hand with the prostitute he had extracted from her windowed street-side room, him going in and out of cannabis shops to make his purchases.

He looked up at Buckrack, his nostrils flaring. "You cunt!" he hissed.

Buckrack blinked and gave a slight gesture of seeming regret. "As I say, it's just one of the things we habitually do. I admit it's not pretty. I could say I am sorry, but you were the guy I told about the bugs. I had no direct contact with Redman or Poon, only with Asterisk in person and you, anonymously, in writing. Asterisk had many of his own self-interested reasons to keep shtum about all this. But I needed to know more about you. I needed to cover my own ass. Of course, I had no idea at all that you were going to become the Vice Chancellor here. That makes this information more powerful now, of course."

"So, what," said McNamara, suddenly flustered, "you're fucking blackmailing me now?"

Buckrack shook his head. "You could look at it another way. What I did with Covet he deserved, and it indirectly led to you now having the position you have. I don't consider you fucking around in Amsterdam and indulging a soft drug habit to be major moral failings. They're even perfectly legal, where you did them. They don't raise you to anything near Covet's level of selfish wickedness. I don't have any beef with you, I have no wish to upset your apple cart the way I did his. All I want to do is protect myself. I don't want anyone connecting me with the buggings, or what did they call it – Odiumgate? I just want your help in keeping my name out of it all."

There was yet another long hiatus. McNamara flushed, inwardly stewing. "And how do I do that?" he said in a defeated tone.

"The problem is Asterisk. He's a coward. He scares easily. He's the one likely to cave in and blab everything he knows. I'd like you to find out what information he may have given to the CID guy, either at their meeting yesterday or since. If he hasn't given them any information, I'd like you to find a way of stopping him doing so. Hopefully he stalled, but he has a habit of trying that at first and then collapsing under pressure."

McNamara considered for a moment. "I suppose I can look into that," he said. He leaned back in his chair and put his hands briefly over his face. He remained in that pose for a moment before revealing his features once more and taking a large breath of air.

To Buckrack's surprise, McNamara gave him a relaxed grin.

"You're good," McNamara said grudgingly.

Buckrack's mouth twisted a little, seeming to acknowledge the perverse irony of this statement.

"But don't you have other problems?" McNamara continued. "Bigger problems than this?"

"Like what?" asked Buckrack.

"Well, for one, the money transaction between Covet and Jane Blake on the night they both died. What was it, fifty thousand dollars?"

"I don't know. I read the news reports, of course," said Buckrack. "There was nothing in them about that."

"Really? You didn't follow the money?"

"Why should I?"

"Didn't you say you made a habit of knowing who you were dealing with?"

"Yeah, but Covet was dead by then. So was she."

"And where were you then? The day they died?"

"What does that matter?"

"I'm curious."

"I was here, in Odium."

"But not for long, seemingly."

"Meaning what?"

"Well, you completely disappeared right about then. The last thing you sent me was, it's true, postmarked the Friday, the same day, or the day after, they died. And yes, it was posted in Odium. But then, all of a sudden, *pouf!*, you're gone. You instantly vanish off the face of the Odium earth, the very same day they died. Where did you go? Where have you been all this time? I have often wondered."

"You don't have to know that."

McNamara gave a slight laugh. "Actually, as your employer, I think I have a right to know." Buckrack said nothing. "Thing is," McNamara continued, "I knew Sir Evan Covet better than you, certainly for much longer than you. I knew Jane Blake also for a fair duration. Not as well as I thought, obviously. Clearly she was ballsier and less seeming-innocent than I could possibly have imagined. She had an exploitative streak in her herself, to be sure, as events have proven. But she was no match for Sir Evan Covet in that respect. No, you're more of a rival to him in the black arts than she was. But of course, before you told me what you just told me, I didn't have you linked with Jane Blake at all in my mind. I just can't see her blackmailing him like that so easily, can you? I can contemplate her doing it with the assistance of someone with a greater genius for blackmail, though."

Buckrack looked calm. "I have no idea where you are going with this. It's a dead end."

"Well, bear with me," said McNamara. "As you know, I didn't take over directly from Covet. There was another guy before me. I certainly witnessed him showing some interest in the events of the previous term. Who wouldn't, right? But I didn't know how much until I succeeded him. And you know what he did? He managed to procure the final police report. It wouldn't have occurred to me that he could even get that, but he was better connected than me, he had friends in higher places. I found it sitting in one of the files in the Vice Chancellor's office. And one of the appendices in that report was a single sheet from Interpol on the bank transaction received a couple of weeks after the deaths. It shows the transfer from Covet's account, made on the Friday night, being cleared in her Boston bank account the following Tuesday, the same account she told us about in her Public Interest Disclosure. But it also shows that this account was virtually emptied the following day, the Wednesday. There was a couple of thousand left in it, but nearly all of it, the fifty grand and quite a lot more, was wired to an investment account in the Cayman Islands."

Buckrack maintained his silence.

"Now how," McNamara asked, "does a young woman, four or five days dead, transfer money out of her account?"

Buckrack gave what appeared to be a humorous chuckle. "The obvious answer is that it was pre-authorised."

"Maybe," said McNamara. "But who pre-authorises such a large transfer before they even have the money? At any rate, the British police didn't like it. Their report noted the oddity. At the time the report was written they recorded that they had made further enquiries and were waiting for a response."

"They closed the case nonetheless."

"Well, yes and no. They agreed with the coroner's verdict of a double suicide on the evidence available but recommended that the case be revised in the light of requested evidence yet to be received. Maybe that new evidence has now been received."

"Or," said Buckrack, "knowing how these things work, maybe the Americans looked into the bank transfer further and that's what piqued their interest. The result's the same. We both agree the case is now being looked at again. I'm not too bothered by the banking issues, and it's the first I have heard of them. I just don't want to get caught up in the new investigation."

"Yes, but I am not entirely convinced by your assumption that this is just Trump causing trouble to vent his bad mood at the University of Odium, because we injured his pride. In fact, I'm not entirely convinced that you yourself believe this. And the reason I am not convinced is that when Trump was on the way here his security detail, the ones who do the clearance in advance of his visit, before we pissed him off, had one guy – CIA, as it turned out – casually asking for information, precisely, about *you*."

For the first time Buckrack's eyelids lowered. "And what did you tell them?" he said.

McNamara smiled gently, and replied, "You don't have to know that. And it wasn't just me they asked. They asked everybody who was going to be anywhere near Trump on the day."

Buckrack cleared his throat. He took a final gulp from his glass. The two stared at each other.

"And how much do you actually know about me, apart from the fact that I went to Amsterdam for recreational drugs and sex?" McNamara went on. "For instance, what exactly is the state of your knowledge as concerns my health?"

Buckrack examined his interlocutor judgmentally for a few moments. "Well, you don't exactly seem in good shape."

"But do I look, for example, jaundiced to you?" McNamara continued.

"No," replied Buckrack.

"Must be the drugs."

"Drugs?" said Buckrack. "For what?"

"Well," McNamara went on, "it's odd, but it'll be good to tell someone at last. Funny, the things you'll say to a stranger. I have pancreatic cancer."

Buckrack was predictably silent.

"You have presumably never tried to blackmail someone before," McNamara said, "and discovered a minute later that they were terminally ill."

Buckrack saw the need at last to say something. "You don't seem to need sentiment, so I'll ask: how long do you have?"

"Weeks, probably," McNamara replied. "Months if I am lucky."

"And the drugs?" Buckrack resumed. "What are the drugs?"

"I can't even pronounce them," McNamara answered. "I just take them. I don't read the label."

"Show me them. Show me the bottle."

"You can eat shit!" McNamara fulminated, looking over the top of his glass. "I don't need to show you anything. It's yet another thing you don't need to know. What you do need to know is that, while I would in a perfect world wish not to go down in dishonour and scandal, my world these days is very far from perfect, as I am going down pretty soon anyway. So I don't really give two tuppenny-ha'penny fucks what you do. There's the door. Blackmail away. Unless you wish to tell me the truth."

Buckrack cocked his head to one side. "The truth?"

"Oh, come on," said McNamara. "I'm not prepared to buy your alleged fear of being roped into an international espionage debacle as sufficient motivation for you following me all the way to Amsterdam six weeks after you disappeared. Sure, I was the guy you sent the bugs to and whom you tipped off, but the whole Trump-CIA thing didn't happen for months after that."

"You forget," countered Buckrack, "that I may have learned about official American interest in the situation long before you did."

"Sure, it's possible," McNamara admitted, "and I can see why anyone wouldn't want to get sucked into the whirlpool. And spooked as I am by being under your surveillance in Amsterdam, common sense tells me you had more personal reasons for keeping tabs on me and supplying yourself with material for blackmail. You had something to hide, something much nastier than planting bugs at the behest of Covet. After all, there was the camera. The one she used to film their sexual assignation, that video you sent me. You gave it to her, right? You got Asterisk to buy it and you gave it to her? It was your idea for her to get evidence with which she could blackmail Covet? It is, after all, we know, don't we, what you do?"

Buckrack remained silent.

McNamara continued. "So, you are in possession of an unsavoury truth about me. You are offering to keep that truth concealed if I take certain steps to hold the police investigation at bay. And yes, I concede that I am not particularly minded to have the case re-examined and all this dirt dragged out into the light of day. But I really don't have to care that much, given that I am dying. And I certainly don't like being blackmailed. So now, why don't you admit to me the unsavoury truth about you? I won't be able to prove it anyway. It'll be your word against mine. You encouraged her to blackmail him, right? You even set the whole thing up?"

Buckrack said nothing.

"You know," said McNamara, "I don't give a damn about Covet or what happened to his money. And once he had killed Jane Blake the money was no good to her anyway. Things went awry for both of them and you somehow, I think, stole the money, right, and that's why you vamoosed? Isn't that the nasty secret you really wish to keep hidden?"

He let a longer silence prevail between them.

After some time, still without saying anything, Buckrack slowly nodded.

McNamara smiled gently. "There, that wasn't so

bad, was it? As I said, it's sometimes good to tell someone." He looked at his empty glass. "So, now that we've traded personal secrets, and know each other better, let's drop all the attempts to cajole by means of threats." He sounded almost jovial. "After all, you're right, I probably wouldn't even be the Vice Chancellor if it hadn't been for you. I didn't exactly not benefit. The pension bump itself is probably more than the sum you stole."

Buckrack sighed a small sigh and said, with seeming sincerity, "Shame you won't get to enjoy it."

"No," said McNamara, "but my beneficiaries will when I die in service. Now, would you like a refill before we discuss further details?"

Buckrack proffered his tumbler. McNamara ambled into the kitchen with it. He stood drunkenly still for a moment, but swaying slightly, only half-remembering why he was there, caught emotionally off-guard by the sudden incongruous domestic quiet of the opulently furnished and gadgeted room. In the end he did not go to the tall, silver-surfaced Fisher and Paykel RF540ADUSX4 Goliath three-door fridge freezer, whose sixty-page user guide had, to his intense irritation, split one of many infinitives while lauding its smart ice maker.[15] Instead, seeing on a rack on the wall Chivers' WNTHBJ 304 stainless steel meat tenderizer – a gleaming hollow-structured device which weighed

---

[15] This is astonishingly accurate. See *ActiveSmart™ refrigerator: Ice & Water and Non-Ice & Water, E372B, E402B, E406B, E442B, E522B, RF522W, RF522A, RF610A & RF540A models* (Fisher and Paykel, 2013), p. 31: "Your ice maker is designed to automatically dispense ice until it senses that the bin is full. So the more ice you use, the more it makes."

just over 700 grams and had both a shallow-nail surface and a deep-nail surface as well as gradual curved handles for a comfortable non-slip grip, and came with a heavy-duty mallet head but no annoyingly American English brochure – he took it firmly in his hand, strode a little lopsidedly back into the living room, and brought it down with full force on the top of Buckrack's skull.

Chapter Six

Perhaps the most unaccountable thing about sudden inexplicable violence is that, while objectively it happens very rapidly (booze-befuddled burly McNamara was to batter bamboozled Buckrack a second and final time with his big-budget beef hammer within barely a blink of the first brawny brain-bash), it seems to take place, in subjective perception, at 600 frames per second. McNamara was thus able to view in wondrous slow-mo hi-def as, with the first blow to the crown of Buckrack's noggin, the American's neck compressed and shot down-down-downwards, while both his shoulders seemed to jerk upwards, then all four limbs jittered reflexively out at once so that the only part of him in contact with the sofa was, for an instant, his pile-driven tailbone. Then, as if it were on a pogo-stick, the head thrust up-up-up again elastically, and conveniently for the now whack-a-mole instincts which had overtaken McNamara, whose twirling right arm was already swinging the top-heavy meat mallet towards it side-on. Its grade 304 stainless steel surface thudded into the top of Buckrack's right ear and his entire body capsized clean over the low armrest of the couch and landed on the carpet, where it commenced silently to twitch then tremble then shiver then convulse like that of a sledgehammered pig McNamara had once seen in a European film, though he could not remember, in his blotto and now incipiently endorphin-influenced state, if it had been directed by Jean-Luc Godard or Bernardo Bertolucci.[16] Fortuitously for the furniture, McNamara had led with the shallow-nail side of the tenderizer. Had he used the deep-nail edge there would most probably have been head pulp on the David Rockwell cream fireside rug and lopped-off fragments of earlobe and antihelix down the back of the white Casa Padrino cushions.

While the ghosts of Leon Trotsky and Joe Orton, wherever they were, no doubt froze in momentary supernatural empathy, McNamara steadied himself with one hand on the back of the sofa and peered curiously over its edge, as one might at a fly one has just swatted with a newspaper and which now lies helplessly quivering on the windowsill.

"You criminal spunkhead," he growled in a low voice. "I'm from fucking Glasgow."

Fortified by this occult, atavistic and neologistic declaration, he turned and went into the hallway and unlocked the cellar door. He returned and, grasping the prone Buckrack by the ankles, dragged him across the carpet.

"Fucking blackmail, eh?" McNamara continued in a monologue directed at the slumped American frame as

---

[16] McNamara is thinking of Godard's *Weekend* (1967). A live pig is also slaughtered in Bertolucci's *Novecento* (1976) but it is unceremoniously disembowelled, not charitably stunned in advance by being poleaxed.

his feet retreated out into the hallway, his arms stretched straight and pulling it laboriously after him. Buckrack's recently bombarded head bumped up and down on the metal base plate of the door at the threshold to the lobby. "You fucking led her right into the lion's den, you cunt. You dickass! You might as well have fucking killed her yourself, you tic-tac shit! You ball-less drosh!" He was running out of breath and cogent insults and had simply begun, unwittingly, to make up pejorative words which fitted in with his faltering respiration. Fricatives and plosives abounded. "You ... frope! You ... brasharse. You ... fucking ... drim!"

At last he got the body to the top of the basement steps. He stepped over it, knelt down, put his arms under the oxters, and heaved the unconscious Buckrack into a sitting position.

"You ... shitfangle!"

Holding Buckrack bent at the waist with a knee propped behind him, McNamara hauled himself up enough to reach the light switch just beyond the door, and waited until the fluorescent tube below flickered into life, casting its stark glare into the white-bricked room. He eased himself further upright, panting with exertion, and as carefully as he could put the sole of his foot in the middle of Buckrack's spine, then pushed.

As the American folded forward and went tumbling, bonce over brogues, like a bowling ball rolled down the alley of the wooden staircase into the depths of the basement, McNamara himself lost balance backwards, staggered woozily, and careered Newtonianly into a thin-legged credenza, hurting his already irksome back.

"Faaaaaaark!" he spat out in pain.

He slumped over the top of the sideboard and got

his breath back. Adrenalin jetted along his veins and whooshed in his arteries, banging at the gates of his heart and making him giddy. Pinpricks of light erupted at the edge of his vision like small exploding stars.

He gathered himself and clambered down the staircase after Buckrack, whom he found hunched up in a crumpled immobile ball, his face on the floor and his arse in the air above the bottom two steps. He pushed the body again with his foot to straighten it out. He leaned down, on all fours, close to Buckrack's face. The biff-costarded man was still breathing.

He found a length of flex in a cupboard and searched for a Stanley knife and cut it in two. One length he wrapped wrist-crushingly tight and tied around Buckrack's joined arms. Then he looped the other length through it and secured it to a wooden support pillar in the middle of the floor, with the double knot on the far side from the now shackled Buckrack. He finally hoisted himself up the stairs breathlessly, holding on to the banister at each step, turned out the light and locked the cellar door from the outside.

He crossed the hallway to the coat stand and had just dug his mobile phone from his jacket pocket when, through the frosted glass of the front door, only a foot away, he saw a flesh-coloured oval shape loom up at face height, then a hand extend to the glass and give three hearty raps.

"Hey, Robert!" he heard Redman exclaim happily, and could even see his smile and his blinks through the blurry window. "Glad you're still up! I'd love a beer! Lots to discuss!"

The sun always rises, on the odious as well as the good. The next morning it peeked above the horizon, clear and bright and promising more great heat, a minute or two earlier than it had the day before. Midway through his fatal morning jog, Professor Adrian Plumb noted (his last professional satisfaction) how its low half-disk cast short shadows down the long sloping field – which most people mistakenly thought of as a manicured lawn – that stretched up towards the Trump Building on the west side, revealing the wave-like shapes of the ancient agricultural furrows made by those who had once had to seek a much simpler existence than his, whose geological exertions he had adverted to in his locally famed topographic tome, and whose once-tilled earth his corpse would enrich within a fortnight.[17]

At a few minutes past nine, about half an hour after Plumb's body had begun to rigidify, unwept for by anyone, in a curtained cubicle in the University Hospital less than half a mile away, McNamara was brought into consciousness with a head non-verbally howling the Book of Ecclesiastes at him and the rest of his body echoing it with a translation in cellular terms of the Book of Lamentations. The cause of his crapulent awakening was his phone trilling at him from the coffee table, and the circumstances of the resurrection, he noted with puzzlement, involved his being fully clothed

---

[17] His gratifyingly bereaved widow, taking some words from An Order for the Burial of the Dead quite literally, put his body to good horticultural use, getting local authority and University permission to bury it intact at the base of her beloved rose bush in the rear garden of their campus home. So Plumb fittingly became part of the very object he had so assiduously researched, so did he flourish as a flower of the field. He thereby joined that small group of the academic elect who not only interpreted the world he studied, but changed it.

and covered with a blanket on the couch in his living room. He stretched for the phone and answered it groaningly without checking who was calling.

To his significant displeasure, it was Elfyn Dethbridge.

"I'm very sorry to disturb you, Vice Chancellor," Dethbridge started saying in his unreformed and hesitant Celtic lilt that made him sound permanently like someone with a low IQ. "But I am in receipt of a document I need to show you immediately. I called your office but you were not there yet."

A few grunted attempts to get Dethbridge to paraphrase the document were met by portentously expressed Welsh negatives and grave claims from deep in the valleys that it could not be discussed on the phone. McNamara reluctantly agreed to let Dethbridge come to his office in an hour. On no account was he going to allow the guttersnipe near his house. He hung up.

He then found himself looking at a box file on the table bearing a sticker on which was printed in bold the word "REDUNDANCIES". Next to it was a pile of photographs, the top one showing him holding the hand of a hesitant Hispanic whore in hallucinatory hash-habit Hamsterdam. Beside that, on top of a closed briefcase, was a note written in pen which read, "Call me when you wake up. James." Before he could reflect on any of these unwanted things, however, the phone painfully went off again.

This time it was an agitated Nigel Asterisk.

"Vice Chancellor, Vice Chancellor, good morning."

"Morning, Nigel."

"Vice Chancellor, I have some disturbing news."

McNamara closed his eyes and put a hand to his

biblically discontented head. "And what's that?" he asked.

"It's Professor Buckrack," Asterisk answered, hardly able to disguise the sense of drama in his voice. "You know who I mean? He's here, he's back in Odium. He called Elfyn Dethbridge yesterday. I don't yet know why."

McNamara was not physically capable of sitting bolt upright but he felt some vague command within his slurrily operating brain stem that suggested he should do so.

"I'll have to call you back, Nigel," he said. "Excuse me. It'll have to wait."

He tossed the phone on the table and struggled to his feet. He walked stiffly out into the hall and turned the key in the lock of the cellar door. The first sign of something amiss was that he did not need to flick on the light. It was already on.

He could see in an instant that Buckrack was no longer in the relatively cramped basement. As he descended the steps slowly his bloodshot eyes took in the obvious signs of an escape. There was a plain, handle-less windowpane above head height, but also just above ground level, which permitted some natural light into the room during the day. It had been smashed from the inside and cleared of splinters so that Buckrack could get through it. As he neared the bottom of the steps McNamara could see that the wire flex with which he had secured Buckrack to the upright pillar had been roughly torn through. As he reached the very last step he smelled urine and saw, contrasting with the floor close to his feet, in a dark bloody puddle, two broken teeth.

*

Our American murderer and blackmailer and avenger and now dentally deprived and incontinent ex-CIA agent has, dear reader, believe it or not, an internal existence just the way you and I have. We would not wish, I am sure, actually to experience his subjective feelings on life (or possible death) just at this moment, but it is perhaps time to do what this triple-decker narrative has so far generally resisted: to explore his unique perspective a little, get behind his eyes and have a look around, and then (as he was to do from the temporarily imprisoning cellar) get the hell out these distressing surroundings after the briefest sojourn.

When those eyes that we are now imagining ourselves behind had opened, they saw nothing at all. Indeed, there was only a glimmer of consciousness, the merest thread of difference, for the first moment, between his couple of hours of violently enforced comatose paralysis and this faint sense that he was still alive. He was incapable of any immediate movement, although he became aware that there was some going on, a shallow rise and fall, in his chest. He was breathing. As moments passed the blackness of his vision commuted into a more graduated greyscale. It was, in fact, a moonlit night, and there was a little illumination in the room from some window somewhere. Then he thought he could hear something. But it was not external sound. It came from two sources in his own body. There was a droning that seemed to originate deep within his skull, which had slowly faded into awareness and then remained at a fixed volume, like an unvarying electric hum, as if a key on an old-fashioned synthesizer had been depressed in there and not released. On the right side of his head, moreover, it sounded as if a conch shell had been placed permanently against his ear, which seemed encased and insulated, and the nerves in his neck just below it seemed constantly to be fluttering, contracting and expanding uncomfortably, producing an unnatural flanging vibration deep within the cochlea, as if an unreal wind were passing to and fro across it. These two aural sensations seemed to act as a screen, making it impossible to discern anything sonic that may be taking place outside them in the room.

He was soon able to reflect on his pitiable plight, both physically and spiritually. To the natural demand for an explanation his affected brain struggled sluggishly but at last successfully to deliver him up a recent memory. He had not been without suffering in his life – he had, after all, once found his own son with a bullet-hole in the back of his throat and a Glock 17 on the floor beside him, in a garage not entirely unreminiscent of this dingy basement (and he had himself, as we know from his dealings with Jane Blake, not been slow to tie people to domestic stanchions when it served his own purposes) – but he had never quite suffered the specific personal shock of being improbably dual-slugged on the nut by a distinguished Professor of Politics. Such sophisticated men did not usually resort instantly to batonic blows to resolve testy disputes the way McNamara had.

Buckrack was feebly knowledgeable that he had enjoyed professional training and lifelong experience which should theoretically have conferred on him an advantage over ordinary mortals in just such a duressful situation. Yet when he tried to remember any particular taught or learned routine, he could summon up nothing useful. He did not know it, but as we have the brief privilege of being behind his eyes we may sweep a narrative light along the top of his concussed brain for an instant and confidently surmise that the bang-bang of McNamara's silver hammer, as it came down upon his head, probably impaired some specific cognitive abilities, perhaps temporarily, perhaps not.

Buckrack fell back on a more primordial propensity: murderous animal instinct. As he took to biting the tough plastic sheath of white flex which shackled him to the pillar, it was his visceral intention, upon releasing himself, to march upstairs and beat McNamara to death where he found him. Even when, after much worrying at the wire, he felt most of his right upper middle tooth crackle, snap and pop out with an accompanying spurt of saliva but no gum blood, he did not find his mind retreating to more sober consequential thinking. Indeed, his immediate reaction was to see it as a fortuitous plus: he would be able to bite a gouge in McNamara's throat much more deeply and painfully with a snaggled toothline than an even one. It was only with the second dental sacrifice that he became more pessimistic as to his chances even of slipping his fetter. This despair began with a premonitory cuspid creaking that seemed to last much longer than it really did in measurable time – as does the discrete instant when one decidedly loses balance and knows one is going to fall – before the canine seemed to fling itself out of his mouth like a fighter pilot ejecting from a doomed plane. Its point of fracture was much deeper than the first. It broke off nearer the root with a disgusting tearing of tissue, sending a hot needle of searing agony up through the nerve into the jawbone that seemed to reach high and lance the bottom of his right eye and make it wriggle and convulse in its socket. The psychic effect was like living a Freudian castration dream. A wave of debilitating impotence crashed over him and he fell prostrate, sobbing and mewling, flat on the floor, with a dim mindfulness that blood was now dripping from his mouth in quantity. As if in sympathy for this liquid loss, his bladder chose that moment to give up the ghost, and he pissed the processed product of McNamara's single malt into his pants.

Minutes passed. He flitted in and out of wakefulness. Impulse told him that time may be in short supply, and he made yet another compulsive effort, taking to gnawing and munching more cautiously, but doggedly, on the now pierced and frayed wire, slavering over it copiously, until, after what seemed an age, he felt the welcome tang of copper coalesce with the iron already in his mouth and, with one last horrible metallic bite, cut through the brittle strands.

From the same wire, wound and tied tightly round his wrists, it was easier to free himself. McNamara had secured it well, but in his sottish state, in which he had never contemplated Buckrack doing a Houdini, he had carelessly left several sharp implements in the basement. Buckrack lumbered to his feet and groped and pawed around the room. He found a light switch on the wall and turned it blindingly on. By this means he found an open toolbox and was able to hold a knife with the handle between his knees and saw slowly through enough of the flex that he could slip his hands from the unsevered, loosened remainder.

He sat for a moment in exhaustion and transient relief, then got back on to his feet. He made for the stairs but discovered within a step that this was to be no triumphal march. He lunged forward, with no control of his centre of gravity, and his left knee gave way under him and came down on the very edge of the first step with a grim crunch, exactly on the reflex point. The pain made him gasp and clutch at the stair rail. He got up and tried to put weight on the leg. The knee answered with injured protest. It did not want to go on any stair-climbing journey after being treated so badly. It turned instantaneously sullen and uncooperative.

Buckrack looked up the steps at the cellar door. It had a mortice lock and opened inwards. Even had his leg been willing, he could not kick it open. If he could find an axe or a hatchet somewhere he might be able to batter a hole in it, but this action would take too much time and he did not know what or who was now on the other side. It would be better to try to get out of the window and take stock from there.

He hobbled back across the room. There was a table beneath the window and, using a chair on which he placed his good leg, he was able to ease himself onto it, despite his tormented knee. He stood gingerly on one foot. His eyeline was now actually a little above the window, his head bowing a little under the roof. The window was recessed a few inches, with a border of masonry above it. It was in two panes, each about twenty inches high and thirty inches across, with a metal frame. He felt confident that his body could fit through it head first. About six inches beyond, across a gravel border, were what looked like shin-high bushes, their tops visible against the ghostly haze of the moonlit night sky.

He looked down for a tool with which he might smash the window, and then sighed with fatigue and futility. He should have picked up something before he had climbed up here, he now realised. The damaged knee was so weak that struggling back down and up presented a prospect of immense, time-consuming agony. Instead, he bent over twingefully and managed to get a hand on the chair and lifted it up onto the table. He put the back of the chair close to the wall under the window and placed his weak knee onto it for support, keeping his other leg straight. He looked at the window and saw his dishevelled, distressed face for a moment palely outlined in reflection, a dark stain of blood all down his chin. Then he braced himself with his hands on the chair back and, using most of the weight of his upper body, dived forward and head butted the right pane of glass in its centre.

He was not sure at first if the crack he heard was the glass or his forehead giving way. In his already concussed state, the bolt of renewed cranial and neck pain was only bearable because it had been anticipated. The humming noise that had been constantly in his skull seemed to leap up in volume for several seconds, but he managed to hold on to the chair and ride the trauma through.

When he looked up again there was a spider-webby shatter pattern radiating out from the middle of the window pane. He was heartened and slightly amazed that, in his present condition, he had calibrated the required impact so accurately. He reached out a flat palm and, still holding the back of the seat with his other hand, while finding that he had to wobble precariously for balance on trembling limbs, applied gently increasing pressure. The glass began to creak and yield until, with the gradually greater stress, it gave way and spilled outward, leaving a jagged hole. He felt slightly cooler air drift in and breathed more hopefully.

He slowly began repeating the procedure nearer the edges of the window, so that bit by bit he was able to clear most of the glass and leave a fairly complete opening. He thought, as he went through, he could most likely avoid the small spars at the top and sides which remained. It was the ones at the bottom of the frame that still concerned him. He could not dislodge these with the ball of his hand. If they were not removed they promised to add stabbing insults to multiple McNamara- and self-inflicted injuries. But he found that if he crooked his arm and used his bony elbow instead of his hand the most prominent of these too could be broken away.

He was relieved, when he now placed both feet on the chair, to discover that with his upper body at right angles to his legs, he could stretch his arms through the aperture he had created and support himself on them while he edged his head, shoulders, chest then stomach guardedly all the way through, keeping them from touching the small, sharp glassy fragments that still clung to the frame. Having gone as far as he could by this method, he rested his hips warily on the inside of the frame, wincing at the barbs he could feel on his front thighs and pelvis. With one hand he stretched and grasped at the root of one of the miniature bushes and tugged at it. It seemed to offer ample resistance. With one fist around it, pulling, and the other hand flat on the soil, alternately levering, he was able to scrape his way laboriously through the escape hatch he had created, with only a few cuts and lacerations to his upper legs.

The katzenjammered Vice Chancellor of the University of Odium was not able to process much by means of sensory data available to him in his now naturally air-conditioned cellar. He decided to return to his living room to call Redman.

"How are you feeling?" Redman asked him.

McNamara searched his memory banks for a phrase that might be meet. "Learish at his worst," he answered, and in the pause that followed found that he was mildly congratulating himself on this erudite, indirect riposte. Perhaps he was regaining his mind. "I mean King, of course, not Edward."

"Do you remember?" Redman asked.

"No," said McNamara. "Total blackout, I'm afraid."

"You fainted," Redman said.

"I fainted?" McNamara repeated.

"Yeah," said Redman. "You opened the door to me, looked in my direction like a wild animal, then just fell in a heap on the floor."

"I did?" said McNamara superfluously.

"You did."

"I was very drunk."

"I gathered."

"Did I say anything?"

"Well, not right then, obviously. And not much later either. I dragged you into the living room. You did resuscitate after a few moments, before I could call an ambulance. What happened?"

"As, I say ... it was just drink."

"Then you were incoherent, for the most part. Jabbering, havering."

"What was I saying?"

"Expletives mainly. *Cunt, fuckhead, wanker*, that kind of thing. I presumed these terms were being used to describe someone other than me. And there were some things that sounded like words but weren't."

"Too much whisky can do that," McNamara said.

"Except for one complete sentence. You started giggling and then said, 'You know what I told him, you know what I told him? I told him I had cancer!' Then you chuckled some more and conked out again. I threw a blanket over you and left the box of redundancy stuff on the table next to the, er, photographs."

McNamara knew that the facts just recited implied questions. But as they were not explicitly stated, he chose to ignore them. "Yes, thanks. Clearly I was talking absolute nonsense. Havering, as you say."

There was no immediate response. Then Redman said, "Okay..."

McNamara filled the gap by answering cordially, "Thank you again. I'll get back to you on the redundancy matters soon."

There was another expectant pause. Nothing rushed in to break it.

Redman finally added, "There was something I meant to tell you. In fact, I would have told you last night. Asterisk had a visit yesterday from the police, asking questions about the Jane Blake murder. He asked me not to say anything to you but I had second thoughts."

"Oh, that," said McNamara. "It's true, then."

"You already knew?"

"Yes," McNamara said. "Asterisk is worried about the fact that the bugs and the camera were procured on his budget by Buckrack."

"So you did know that it was Buckrack who planted the bugs?"

"Not until yesterday, not for sure," McNamara replied.

Redman said, "Oh."

"I'll talk to Asterisk. Do me a favour. Don't tell him you told me."

Thus their conversation faltered to an end.

*

Buckrack was quick to discover that his life had been divided into two parts. There was the life he had had before McNamara repetitively clattered his capitulum, and now a kind of parody of that life afterwards.

Once he exited the cellar, all thoughts of returning to the scene of the warningless assault evaporated. Instant revenge was not now the priority: base survival was. He could hardly stand upright. His body kept tilting naturally to the left, putting the weight on his damaged knee, and he could stay erect only by deliberately counter-leaning to the right, which felt entirely abnormal and made his first few experimental steps freakishly teetering and uncertain.

At the back of his mind, behind the continuing humming in his brain, was now another constant buzz of unanswered speculation. He could not fathom why McNamara had set about him so viciously and forcefully. Confining him in the cellar afterwards and tethering him there had been done, presumably, with the intent of calling the police, and while there was as yet no sign of their having been summoned, the very prospect meant that he needed to quit the environs of McNamara's house as rapidly as his malfunctioning body would allow.

As he hobbled away, with each short step the vast extent of his distressful vulnerability was borne in upon him. He was entirely alone and seriously injured. His own outlaw actions meant that he himself could hardly solicit aid. He was not CIA now, and no extraction team would be swooping in on a Black Hawk to carry him away from the theatre of operations. He could hardly go to an emergency ward for treatment and care; if McNamara did summon the authorities and inform them of what had happened, such a place would be the first they would look.

The one bolthole he had within immediate reach was his campus home, though it was unlikely that he could stay there safely for very long. But it was the middle of the night and he could perhaps risk sheltering there for an hour or two, enough time to grab some personal things, clean himself up and make away in slightly better shape. But he had lost all sense of orientation. He was not sure in which direction his house was from here.

He halted, propping himself against a tree trunk, and managed to ease his phone out of his trouser pocket. He could use GPS to find the way. A moment later he was looking at the screen indecisively. The oddest thing was that it did not seem to be in colour. It looked flatly monochrome, its usually vibrant hues absent. This could hardly be a trick of the light. He was standing in a dark, sheltered arbour. Perhaps it had been damaged when McNamara manhandled him. But he had little time to consider the anomaly.

The first attempt to enter his passcode failed. He saw that the fingers of his right hand were trembling. He switched to his left but found this even less nimble. It was numb in all the digits, which were difficult to control. When he held it up and shone the faint pearly light of the phone screen upon it, it appeared to be fixed in an inflexible semi-claw shape. He cradled the phone back into his left hand and, with more deliberation, poked at the numbers on the screen with the extended index finger of his right. At the third digit his mind went vacant and he stood for several seconds in a forgetful mental miasma. He searched for the desired four-number series in his head, and then began to doubt the accuracy of even the first two. He nonetheless stabbed hopefully twice more at the screen and completed the sequence, but it failed. He tried again and was still incorrect. Halfway through the third bid he prodded hard enough to unmoor the phone and send it slipping out of his weak left hand to fall on the tree roots at his feet. Bending down to retrieve it was a painful trial.

And then some welcome vestige of his professional training seemed to ping in his impaired thought processes. The phone now was nothing but a liability. It could be tracked. He prised the back off with less than cooperative fingers, removed the SIM and the memory card and battery, and put them in his pocket.

He staggered forth, dumping the phone in a nearby litter bin, seeking in the distance for some landmark which might give a clue to the route home. Something told him that he should head over the brow of the hill he was on, where there was a large sloping grassy area with student halls of residence at the bottom of it. He was relieved to discover that he was right. Once he gained a vantage point from which he could overlook the downland, he was able to see a paved path which bisected it, because its line was traced out by a string of lampposts shining above it on either side.

He stepped gratefully forward and his foot immediately caught in stout rushes, and he bundled over headlong into a thicket of nettles. His chest heaved and wheezed with the smarts these imparted to his face and the bone-shuddering effect of the tumble. He lay quiescent for a few minutes, not only stung and aching, but now knowingly scared at his unaccustomed helplessness and fragility. He thought of simply remaining there and receding into a welcome sleep. But his frightened impulses would not let him. He dragged himself to his feet and stumbled on.

In this way he made the slow journey of about half a mile, sometimes veering somnambulistically off course to the right for twenty or thirty yards at a time before correcting himself, tripping and falling three times on the way, eventually getting close to his house after pursuing a bearing which was whatever the opposite of a bee-line is.

Twenty yards away from the front door, he saw through one of the windows the distinctive arcing beam of a torch moving inside the house. He stopped short and lumbered to the side of the brick building, edging around the sturdy bushes which sheltered the back garden to a point at which he could take in the entire rear of the building. He saw the torch flash again several times behind the curtains of the upper floor rooms. Finding standing dreadfully uncomfortable, he crouched down in the darkness. But this too proved impossible to suffer for long, and so he lay down on his side on the narrow pebbly ditch which bordered the garden, keeping watch on the house through the railings.

And in that position, a few minutes later, he fell asleep. He had his one painless ear to the ground, but he did not hear what was coming.

Chapter Seven

McNamara could not have supplied anyone with a suasive explanation for his unbidden binate blitzkrieg on Buckrack's bodily belfry. He could not adequately account for it to himself, as he downed an entire carton of orange juice, took two multivitamins, a couple of Panadols and one five-hour energy capsule, but no pancreatic cancer medication.

His drastic action of the night before had not been premeditated. McNamara had discovered himself in his kitchen, excessively drunk and mountingly irate, ostensibly fetching ice for Buckrack's nightcap one minute, but delivering something a bit more like an icepick to Buckrack's skullcap the next. He remembered bellowing something absurd at Buckrack's unconscious carpeted form about having grown up in Glasgow. There was in fact some essential truth in this utterance, but only insofar as it was a kind of shorthand vindication of a primal reaction. Buckrack's black-mailing habits, which were usually no doubt the castings of a skilled angler into ponds of deep personal insecurity, had on this occasion been incautiously exercised near sulphuric waters, toxified by whisky and McNamara's complicated feelings about Jane Blake.

The confidently fishing Buckrack had not drawn forth the merely modest catch he sought, but instead had provoked a teratoid Moby-Dick of fury and ferocity, which had surged clean up out of the depths and landed on the bank, crushing the unprepared piscator mercilessly.

It was this demonic spontaneity, issuing in bestial force, which most troubled McNamara, as he trudged into the Trump Building after having showered and dressed. Not for the first time, he was forced to reckon on something within himself which he had previously considered to be the very seed of evil at work in Sir Evan Covet. Had not his predecessor suffered the same lack of civilised restraint when he plunged a blade into Jane Blake's belly? Did the office of Vice Chancellor of the University of Odium now carry some primeval curse with it which ensured that it was nasty, brutish and short? Was the Trump Building really a veiled House of Usher whose master was condemned to a foreseeable doom?[18]

Elfyn Dethbridge was waiting for him in Meifeng's outer office. Meifeng smiled broadly and without repr-

---

[18] Not for the first time, our narrator is Poe-faced. In the Gothic tale, Roderick Usher is withering away spiritually and physically in his "mansion of gloom", grieving at the death of his "lady Madeline". The romance of Ethelred ("who was now mighty withal, on account of the powerfulness of the wine which he had drunken ... uplifted his mace, and struck upon the head of the dragon, which fell before him") seems to hover prophetically over Usher and the house, and both eventually fall "victim to the terrors he had anticipated". The house eventually disintegrates into the earth, with Usher's dead body inside it. The reader interested in how the presaged end of Odium is to occur need hardly read on. Take ye heed: behold, I have foretold all things.

oach at McNamara's arrival: she did not, then, appear to be in a mood of censure on account of anything in his behaviour the previous evening. Dethbridge, he knew, lived in a permanent state of private animus towards him, yet seemed more than ever today his usual cowed and deferential self. McNamara had discovered that it was not easy, as Vice Chancellor, to know if staff thought ill of you or not. Many of them did a little performance when in his presence rather than conducting themselves according to nature. Some seemed to find it difficult even to meet his eye, as if he were a Japanese Emperor or they would thereby be doing something akin to looking directly at the sun. So he never could quite tell what they were genuinely thinking.

He gestured Dethbridge into his inner sanctum and the Welshman, he reflected with apparent prejudice, obeyed with all the seeming pleasure of something entering his inner rectum. Then he waited, standing like a schoolboy in the headmaster's office before accepting McNamara's express invitation to sit.

McNamara was not in daily life a genuine homophobe, not a regular gay- hater or baiter or slater. His younger son was gay, and McNamara loved him without gayness ever being a detrimental feature in their emotional equation. No, with Dethbridge his revulsion was decidedly *a posteriori* rather than *a priori*. It was some obsequious, crawling, creeping, servile factor in Dethbridge's very being, he thought, which seemed to bring his otherwise incidental homosexuality into associative disrepute. And so, unsurprisingly, in their present encounter McNamara found distasteful what he always found distasteful about Dethbridge, namely every single thing, each nuance of behaviour, from his mannerisms to his tones, from his facial expressions to his word choices, from the way he held himself awkwardly in his body to his false fawning before authority. This sour, rotten soup of detestable personal attributes, served up in an earthen bowl of bland Welshness bearing a floral pattern of awkward queerness, as McNamara saw it, did not activate pre-existing Taffy-bashing tendencies or inbuilt faggot-rancour but, instead, seemed to call these responses forth with all the naturalness one would expect in any person whose appetite, gustation and palate operated within the standard, well-adjusted human range.

Dethbridge, always vainly trying to charm, seemed to radiate harm; his constant attempts to insinuate himself led you to wish to exterminate his self; if he tried to nurse you he would curse you; he was more hex than sex; a poisonous infiltrator posing as a poised administrator; a mortal gallstone, not a moral lode-stone; more cellular spatter than well-formed molecular matter. For the terms that adequately pinned down his essence you would have to consult an expansive historical dictionary – one with words in it like *varlet*, *caitiff* and *scofflaw*. His soul was a small dark blob made of an as-yet undiscovered, highly unstable element: odiumite.[19]

---

[19] I ask the typically unreflective reader to make an unusual effort and speculate where we are positioned narratologically by these prolonged, digressive, very unprosy sentences: presumably inside McNamara's hungover sensibility? One likewise wonders, on the other regular occasions when the text excurses into obtrusive alliteration and childish rhyming, if we are not hearing a kind of

"This document was delivered to me in my office by hand just after nine this morning," Dethbridge was saying as he pulled a sheaf of papers out of an envelope he held. "But although it was addressed to me, it's not for me. It appears to be directed at the University."

McNamara reached over and took the document, looked at it briefly, and felt his neck hairs stand on end.

"Why was it delivered to *you*?" he asked with undisguised distrust, looking up at Dethbridge piercingly.

Dethbridge was wide-eyed innocence in adult human form. "That I don't know. But as it *was* addressed to me, I'm afraid I did read it. It's a writ, yes? And all I can guess about why it was served on me is that it mentions both you and the Registrar by name, though I don't understand what difference that should make. But this is why I called and asked to see you urgently."

McNamara blinked at Dethbridge for a few seconds. Then he said, as coolly as he could, "I don't think it's called a writ these days. It's merely a claim form submitted as part of a civil action. We get these from time to time, you know, damaged property, personal injuries, students suing us for their academic failure, mostly trumped-up stuff. But obviously it's confidential, and you should speak to no one else about it. Thank you for bringing it to me so quickly."

---

demented babble, short holidays taken away from good sense, the uncontrollable upfrothing of senile language onto a surface customarily smooth and well managed, caused by perturbations in the invisible depths below, fractures in the supportive crust, which as they multiply and extend surely point ahead to an almighty eschatological crack-up and collapse?

Dethbridge got to his feet. The meeting had lasted barely a minute. "If there's anything else I can do..."

McNamara nodded. "I'll let you know."

But then, as Dethbridge was making to leave, McNamara called him back.

"There was, now it occurs to me, one other thing," McNamara said.

"Yes?" replied Dethbridge expectantly.

"I understand you had a call yesterday from Professor Buckrack."

Dethbridge's reaction was nonchalant. "Yes, I did."

"What did he want?"

Dethbridge shrugged. "He wanted to talk to the Registrar. But it was late in the day, about 6pm. I assumed the Registrar had left and he was put through to me by, er, default."

"But what did he say?"

Dethbridge looked puzzled. He found himself shifting his weight a little from foot to foot. "He didn't say anything. When he realised it was not the Registrar he was speaking to, he simply asked me to tell Nigel he had called, which I did."

"Funny," remarked McNamara, unblinkingly.

"Funny?" Dethbridge repeated.

McNamara looked at him levelly, with a straight stare. "Funny that within such a short space of time you should be the conduit for two communications to those above you in the hierarchy." Then he scanned Dethbridge's face for signs of reaction, for any tinge of confessed guilt in the cheek or twinge of acknowledged nefariousness in the muscles.

But there were none. Instead Dethbridge simply pouted a little thoughtfully and shook his head. "I couldn't have spoken to him for more than twenty seconds. Who is Professor Buckrack anyway? I don't even know of him. He didn't say what his business was."

McNamara relented, then decided, with great effort, to try to sound emollient. "It's okay. Sorry. Listen, Elfyn. We have had our differences, I know. I'd like to be able to put those behind us. We are about to enter a difficult period. I am going to have to rely on the discretion and good sense of people like you in senior management. You'll see why soon enough. So I don't want there to be any hard feelings between us about things in the past."

The Welshman looked pleased. He smiled a little, constrained smile. "Of course, Vice Chancellor," he said. "I will do whatever is needed."

Once Dethbridge had gone, Meifeng came with yet another document, ensuring that his daily treadmill of bureaucratic reading continued to grind without let-up.

"This is Mrs Scheep's final version of the redundancies letter, Vice Chancellor, incorporating your amendments. She has already signed it. If you would like to check it over and sign it if you approve, I will have it emailed to all staff within the hour."

"Okay," said McNamara. "Thank you. I will read it now." Then, with a glance at the papers Dethbridge had delivered, he added, "Would you please contact the Registrar and ask him to come and see me as soon as he can after ten-thirty?"

Meifeng left, and McNamara turned his gruff attention and his migrainous morning-after mind to the six-page letter which was to spell out occupational catastrophe later that day for over five hundred employees. He finally added his signature to that of Surya Scheep, the Chief Financial Officer, and called

Meifeng to fetch it.

"The Registrar is coming in a few moments," she said as she was leaving. "Shall I send him straight in?"

"No, give me ten minutes. Ask him to wait. I'll call you when I am ready."

McNamara spent the ten minutes reading the papers Dethbridge had brought. Then he called Meifeng back in a mood worse than his headache.

Asterisk blustered in, and started speaking instantly, and a little dramatically, as if the meeting were being held at his request.

"Bad news, I'm afraid," he began.

"You don't say," McNamara rejoined.

"It's Professor Plumb. He's dead."

"Adrian Plumb?"

"Yes."

"But I was just talking to him here in this office yesterday. He seemed to be under the impression that this building was going to fall into the lake."

"What?"

"Never mind."

"I got a call from his department. He didn't turn up to his nine o'clock lecture this morning. They called his private number. Someone told them he'd been taken to the University Hospital suddenly. Heart attack, apparently, at home."

"Jesus," said McNamara in a low voice.

"You will want me, of course, to make arrangements, contact his wife – "

"No. I'll deal with that. There was something else."

"Yes." Asterisk's judgment was again wayward. He seemed to think he had just been asked a question. "It's Professor Stoner. He's also in hospital, but he's not dead."

"What? William Stoner?"

"Appears he was mugged early this morning, cracked over the head, assailant stole his wallet. One of the campus residents found him, luckily knew who he was. He's still unconscious, in intensive care."

McNamara scratched his head. "Fuck. I'll contact the hospital."

"I can do that, if you like."

"No, Nigel, William's a close friend of mine. In any case, we need to talk, you and I."

"Oh."

"About yesterday."

"Ah yes, Professor Buckrack."

"No, not about Professor Buckrack. Well, indirectly. Did you try to call him back yet?"

"No. He didn't leave a number. I don't have a working number for him."

"Well, don't try. But on the subject of Buckrack, you have never really been candid with me, Nigel, have you?"

"What do you mean? I did tell you about him stealing the evidence of the bugs."

"Oh yes, you did that. You just didn't tell me that he planted them in the first place, and that he also gave Jane Blake the video camera she made the sex video with. Oh, I'm not stupid, Nigel. I wondered for a long time how Buckrack knew all about the bugs in my office, Redman's and Poon's. And over time I clicked that he – not Jane Blake –must have put them there. But now I also know what I didn't know, what you didn't care to tell me: that they were bought on your budget with your knowledge. You remember that night in the University club? The night you came in worried about the guy in the Secret Service entourage, the one you thought might be CIA, who showed you a picture of Buckrack and wanted to know if you knew him? I asked you directly if it was Jane Blake who planted the bugs. Your answer was, 'Didn't she?' You made out that she did it in collusion with Covet. And yet you knew fine well she didn't."

Had it not been for the Valium he had popped an hour before, Asterisk would now have been edgy, his eyes darting nervously around in their sockets. Instead he seemed to sag. "I, I ..."

"You *what*?" McNamara spat. "You *lied*, right? You lied to my face."

Asterisk gulped. "But you weren't Vice Chancellor then."

"I am now. And you have lied by omission since I became so. You kept me in the fucking dark."

"But ... but ... it had all blown over. It was history."

"Well, it's not history now. I've got a bloody notice of a private prosecution in my hands. We – the University – are being prosecuted by the family of Jane Blake. By her mother, to be precise. She is attempting to prove our culpability for actions leading to the homicide of her daughter. Count one, our employee, namely Sir Evan Covet, murdered her. But count two, a named person allegedly colluded with Covet in conduct which assisted him in doing so: you, by purchasing listening devices that recorded her conversations when she was in Poon's office and my study, as well as the now missing video camera used to film their sexual encounter. And count three, two other named persons cooperated with you in concealing the existence of the bugs: me and James Redman. There's an affidavit from Avril Poon in here swearing that we did so. Now, I don't know, Nigel. I suppose Ms Blake's own written confession of her prostitutional activities and getting herself into mortal danger by such means may count against her reputationally in court. I guess Poon's sexual proclivities, especially as they manifested themselves towards Ms Blake, if they have to come out, may discredit Poon also, although we both know that what Poon says in her affidavit is essentially true. We gave you back the original invoices for the supposedly non-existent bugs. We kept copies and the very much existent bugs themselves. We never mentioned any of this to anyone. I'm not sure what your defence is going to be for buying them on your budget, though. And worst of all, this either costs us a packet to settle out of court – and to do that we'd need the approval of University Council, from whom we can hardly conceal this private prosecution the way you did the original Odiumgate affair – or the entire institution, and its two most senior officers, you and me, as well as Redman, get dragged through the mud in a courtroom trial. And yet you sit here and still don't tell me the whole truth."

"But I ... I can't believe this."

"You were visited by the CID yesterday! You weren't going to let me know, were you?"

"I ... I see ... James must have told you."

"I didn't learn about it from Redman. But you informed him and not me?"

"I was asking for his advice. It was only yesterday. I didn't see you."

"Oh, you were going to tell me today, were you? Now, don't fucking lie to me any more, Nigel."

"I was taking a period to think. I needed a little time. I was trying to find a way round the problem. But wait. If James didn't tell you, how do you know?"

"That's irrelevant."

Asterisk thought he had caught on to something. "Wait. Wait … are you bugging *my* office now? I didn't tell anyone except Redman. You couldn't possibly know if he didn't tell you."

"Don't be absurd. I am not bugging your office. What the fuck is wrong with you? You were the one who conspired in a bugging scandal, not me."

Asterisk's eyes were like small wide pools. He seemed half way to paranoia already. "But you must be. It's the only explanation. It's impossible otherwise. No one but Redman knew about Nesbit coming to see me yesterday."

"It doesn't matter how I know. I know. I'm the Vice Chancellor, for god's sake. I know things. But I don't know because I bugged your office. The idea is insane. And it's not the main thing anyway. You didn't tell me about it, that's what matters. Why didn't you?"

Asterisk's mind was slowly burrowing its way into the desperateness of his position. "I needed time to figure out a solution."

"A solution to what?"

"The CID guy, Nesbit, he wanted to look at our purchasing records. I said he could, knowing he wouldn't find anything. The paper invoices for the bugs and the video camera are no longer in my departmental files. But no, he wanted permission to look at the electronic records of our suppliers. If he did that, well, he'd find the invoices on my budget for the video camera and the three listening devices, and then he'd come back at me and know I had been lying, and the whole affair would be blown wide open again. So I said I would need to run the request past you and get back to him."

"And why didn't you?"

"Why didn't I get back to him?"

"No, why didn't you run the request past me?"

Asterisk looked awkward. "Well, I told him I wouldn't see you 'til today. And I suppose I am now running it past you."

McNamara slapped an intemperate hand on his desk and Asterisk jumped a little in startlement in his seat. "But you *weren't going to run it past me*, were you? You didn't come here now to *run it past* me. You came to talk about Buckrack. Just like when you called me this morning it was to tell me about Buckrack. You had *no fucking intention* of telling me about this. You were looking for what you call a solution. What did you have in mind?"

Asterisk hesitated, then said timidly, "I was trying to get round the difficulty he posed. We couldn't stop him doing the search, he could get a warrant, but I wondered if there was some way of ..."

His words petered out.

"Some way of *what*?"

"Some method of putting him off the scent ... of frustrating his search ..."

McNamara banged the desk even harder and Asterisk jumped a little higher.

"Some way," hissed McNamara through clenched teeth, "of not cooperating, of covering up the truth with a lie, or a deception, or a distraction! Exactly. Your whole fucking *modus operandi*! Conceal the truth to save your own neck!"

"But, but ... I was thinking about the position it would put the University in, not just myself."

"Oh, you fucking lying, short-sighted, pathetic little *cunt*!" McNamara snarled. "You half-created the position the University is in yourself with all your earlier lies! And now you want not only to keep me in the dark but to deceive the police when they are investigating a murder committed by the man who was at the head of this organisation! You think that is a solution! How much of a witless imbecile are you?"

Asterisk sat sheepish and silent. He could hold McNamara's enraged accusatory stare for less than a second or two.

With flaring nostrils, McNamara leafed through a few pages on his desk before him, and his tone turned judicial. "And now I have to clean up the shambles of your making. So let me tell you, and for once I hope you can face reality: you're finished, unless I can find some means of making this prosecution go away quietly. If I can't, I shall have to take the matter to University Council, either to approve an out-of-court settlement or make a decision to contest it. I have lost all confidence in you. I cannot trust you to be honest, not to conceal vital matter, or even to exercise the basic duty of care your office demands. You appear to have lost all proper professional judgment. And while that is the case, I will not have you where you can do any further damage. You are therefore suspended on full pay, pending potential disciplinary action. I will consider your case further in the next few days. You will hear from me at home by letter. You will leave this building immed-iately. You will talk to no one before you do so. You will not contact Detective Superintendent Nesbit on the matter of our purchasing records. I will do that. If he contacts you, you will cooperate with him truthfully. You will not be allowed on University property until further notice. If you disobey any of these injunctions, you will be summarily dismissed. Your suspension will be treated in the strictest confidence. Do you understand all I have said to you?"

Asterisk had sat through this monologue of simmering wrath in an increasingly cowed manner, his face gradually adopting the lineaments of chastened meekness, his Adam's apple moving up and down, his eyes becoming moist. Now he said, deferentially, "Yes, Vice Chancellor. Do you want his card?"

"Whose?" said McNamara.

"The policeman's. Nesbit."

"I don't need it," McNamara said dismissively. Then, to rub it in, he went on. "As you are aware, I already met him when I identified the bodies, something I told you about long ago while you still went on withholding material information from me. I know where to contact him."

Asterisk swallowed. "Okay, Vice Chancellor."

"But before you go," said McNamara, "you came here to talk to me about Professor Buckrack. So you will tell me, right now, everything you know about him, what you are aware that he did, your interactions with him, your conversations about him with Covet, every last whole goddamn jot and tittle, that's what I want, every particle of information you have on the man. And you will answer every question I ask you about these things. You got that?"

"Yes," Asterisk croaked, "Vice Chancellor."

McNamara sat back in his chair.

"Then begin," he commanded.

Chapter Eight

The grilling took an hour, by the end of which McNamara was convinced he had bled Asterisk dry, and despatched him. He then noticed that his headache had blissfully disappeared, the performance of power and enforcement of fear on his detested Registrar seeming to act like a welcome analgesic.

But the new things he learned about Buckrack did not seem terribly useful, in the present situation, in helping decide what to do about him. Asterisk knew little about Buckrack's dealings with Covet and nothing about his interactions with Jane Blake. Buckrack's behaviour towards Asterisk, as told – his bullying and intimidation, his entirely minatory bearing – sounded convincing and familiar. Hearing of the mechanics of how Buckrack had come to Asterisk's assistance and removed the purchase invoices from his office files did not substantially enlarge McNamara's already first-hand knowledge of the American's ruthless skill in cover-up and deception.

He sat for some minutes doing something he did frequently: making a list of people he needed to see to address efficiently the list of issues that daily arose, which he would then pass to Meifeng, who would summon them to an instant meeting or get them on the phone.

Today's problems had rapidly grown to look like vexatious trials, intractable enormities. He had thought it would be tricky enough with just the redundancy missive going out. It was no doubt already causing startle-eyed reactions as the PDF attachment it came in was being scrolled incredulously down screens across campus. But now there was the additional problem of having received formal notice of an imminent private prosecution of the University. And he had just had to suspend his untrustworthy Registrar, whose multifarious functions, including dealing with the hot telephone calls that would start flooding in about the redundancy letter that very afternoon, needed quickly to be assigned to someone else. On top of that, he must decide without delay what to do about the renewed CID investigation. And to cap it all, the common denominator in these cumulatively avalanching and tormentingly beknotting difficulties was Buckrack, the unpredictable Buckrack, whom he had unthinkingly beaten up and held captive the night before, but who had escaped, was now a loose Cannon, and would do what unaccountable crazy shit next?

Something began to nag at the back of his mind as he made the list. Asterisk had wondered how McNamara had known about the visit of the CID officer. McNamara had not known until Buckrack told him the previous night. He had had it confirmed by Redman in their phone call that morning, but Redman had heard it directly from Asterisk. This left an unanswered question: how had Buckrack known? And how had he found out so quickly, so instantly, on the very day?

And then a horrible suspicion began to form in his mind. He picked up the phone. "Meifeng, would you get me the Head of Security, Jagger Harmwell? I need to speak with him immediately. Then please contact Elfyn Dethbridge. I need to see him now, or as soon as possible, and definitely before lunchtime. I also need you to call the University Hospital intensive care department and ask them about the condition of Professor William Stoner and let me know what they say. If he is conscious, please book a car to take me there around one o'clock. Then I need to see, as early as possible from two o'clock onwards, Dr Avril Poon in Cultural Studies. And, oh yes, could you also please let me have the next-of-kin contact details for Professor Adrian Plumb in the School of Earth Sciences..."

Nigel Asterisk, as he slunk out of McNamara's office, had decided to reassume a path he knew well and had strayed from only to his peril, that of obedience: not simply his chronic, habitual adherence to the edicts of whatever Vice Chancellor happened to be in place in the University of Odium that term (the position by now having become an alarmingly fast-rotating kaleidoscope of the shifting obsessions and arbitrary whims of its various post-holders) but to the much larger dictates of fate also. For against the cruelties of that capricious force he had at least made provision.

Stopping in his office only to pick up his jacket and his briefcase and his bubble pack of Valium from his desk drawer, he glid past his secretary in her outer office without word of explanation as to his leaving, as McNamara had specified he should, and went straight to the car park. He sat behind the wheel for a few moments, and experienced a small positive impulse he could not have bargained on, something one could not quite call relief, but an easement all the same, a kind of consolation, a feeling that the very worst was over and that whatever else was to come could not possibly be as bad. It had something to do with the expiation of the confessional. He had at last been able, even if under compulsion, to unburden himself of his secrets to McNamara. The current Vice Chancellor was in a state of unruly apoplexy towards him, and there was no blaming him for that. But it might pass in a little time if Asterisk remained compliant and untroublesome: give way enough, perhaps, for McNamara to accept his resignation rather than put him through the ordeal of a disciplinary procedure and ignominious dismissal.

As he reversed his car carefully out of its space and set off down University Drive, steering it carefully and with now accustomed sensitivity to being under the influence of a powerful tranquilliser, he awarded himself a gold star for being fifty-seven years old. While he acknowledged that no one deserves praise for this fact, because it involves little more effort than managing to stay alive, being above fifty-five meant that he could take a reduced occupational pension on early retirement any time he liked. He also considered that he deserved top marks for not being married, even though the faintest flicker of an opportunity to attain such a condition had never arisen in his entire span of existence.[20] But his enforced bachelorhood (which had in the past been a source of great personal insecurity

***

[20] Had it done so, we might with little doubt have expected – given Clockman's tendency towards broad farce in names – his wife to be called Hyphen, his son Colon, and his daughter Ampersand.

and anxiety) now spared him the necessity of divulging his present disgrace to a spouse awaiting him at home, or of concerning himself with the financial reper- cussions that it might otherwise have visited on the dependants which would probably have been the fruit of his and a wife's conjoined loins. For years, now, he had been maxing-out on advance voluntary contribut- ions to his pension fund. There had still been plenty left over from his six-figure salary to plough with un- interrupted regularity into a now formidably obese unit trust.

After ten minutes, he drew up in the drive of his three-bedroom detached home in a posh suburban cul- de-sac, the mortgage repaid in full a couple of years ago, now owned by him outright, the final badge of honour in his totally successful private pursuit of pecuniary prudence. Celibacy, property, pension: the legs of a redoubtable tripod which the vagaries of even the baddest karma would be unlikely to rock.

It was with this mollifying meditation that he pressed the remote on his keypad and watched the electric garage door tilt up smoothly so that he could roll the car into the empty space. With the added prospect of kicking back with more Valium whenever he felt like it, he unlocked the door in the garage wall that gave access to his hallway, stepped inside, cast his briefcase on the floor, and began to take off his jacket.

The door swung to and closed softly, pneumatically. For a few seconds he breathed in reassuring domestic air and savoured comforting household scents.

Then an American voice sounded from his rear, a voice he had heard before, from the blind spot which had been behind the door when he opened it. "Hey there, fatso."

He twisted around, his hands still holding the lapels of his jacket at the shoulders, and managed to cry out only "Oh my – !" before the flattened fist of Buckrack's right arm crashed into the middle of his face.

McNamara got through some of his to-do list. He managed to speak to Adrian Plumb's widow and briefly conveyed his condolences. He had in Elfyn Dethbridge, and to the visibly dilating pupils of the Deputy Registrar, informed him that Asterisk was unwell and would be absent for a spell, and that he needed him to act in his senior's place. Dethbridge's alacrity was fulsome, though he expressed a seemingly conditional keenness to take up residence in Asterisk's actual office. McNamara was not in a mood to cavil but, with an eye to what he wished to consult Jagger Harmwell about before then, put him off until four that afternoon. This was good enough for Dethbridge, who had to resist the urge to skip out of the room. Then McNamara called Harmwell and set up a meeting for 1.45pm.

By 1.07pm he was being swooshed into the University Hospital VIP car park by his driver, Brian Blackfoot, in the University Lexus, and by 1.14pm he was stepping through the doors of William Stoner's room in intensive care.

Stoner was awake but dazed, feebly irritable but grateful to be visited. His head was vastly bandaged: the fabric had been rolled under his chin and around both his ears as well as all over the top of his head, leaving only a U-shaped portion of his face visible. He was sitting upright, aided by a stout white neck brace, which, along with the cream hospital gown, enhanced the illusion that he had adopted a medical variant of a hijab.

"Still dressing all in white, I see," McNamara quipped. "What happened?"

Stoner grumbled. "It's what I get for playing the Good Samaritan. I was walking in, early, as I do, on that path near the Sports Centre. There are two cottages just there, you know, they back on to it. I thought I saw something in the kind of sloping ditch by the fence that surrounds them and I walked over, and sure enough, there's this poor chap, lying on his side, unconscious, seemingly, with a great welt on his ear, massive blue and black bruising and purple swelling on the side of his head, the front of his trousers all torn and bloody. I thought at first he might be dead. He'd clearly been in some sort of fracas. So I got down and spoke to him but there was no response. I put my hand on his shoulder and gave him a gentle shake. His eyes opened. He was a little bewildered, scared maybe. Then, all in a second, he lurched up, with a stone in his hand, and he thumped me on the skull with it. Didn't say a word. Next thing I know I'm in here four hours later with a police constable sitting where you are. Bastard stole my wallet and my trousers, apparently. Left me in my damned underwear."

"Good grief," McNamara extemporised. "We might have some cameras there, you know. I can ask security. Do you have the policeman's number?"

His friend gestured at a card on the bedside cabinet. "Won't do my bloody head any good," he lamented. "Stoner stoned, you might say."[21]

---

[21] Indeed, he has ironically become the very man the Good Samaritan helped, whose thieving assailants "stripped him of his raiment, and wounded him, and departed, leaving him half dead" (Luke 10, 30).

McNamara remained another ten minutes to give sympathy and consolation.

Asterisk did not quite become the second person Buckrack rendered unconscious that day. The punch to the middle of his face did not lay him out, but sent him flailing backwards, as a consequence of which his head bounced against the lobby wall and his awareness and vision went immediately all fuzzy and dissociated. He had a sense of being bundled to the floor then dragged by the ankles, his mouth and chin wet with blood from his nose that got into his mouth and made him splutter and heave.

This activity soon stopped and he was left still. He eventually gathered that he was on the tiled floor of the small windowless utility room off his kitchen, with his head near the tiny doorstep at its entrance, the open door to his right, a washing machine and tumble drier on his left, and a large blue plastic laundry basket at his feet. When he arched his neck backwards to look, he saw the upside-down form of Buckrack, looming over him just outside the door frame, holding one hand to the side of his head, a large kitchen knife in the other.

"Just you stay there," Buckrack instructed, pointing the tip of the knife in his direction. "Don't you move. If you behave yourself I'll get a cushion for your head. If you don't I'll cut your fucking throat."

Asterisk had already resolved that obedience was

One is tempted to see this entire campus trilogy as a similar parody of the parable, in which a nobly intentioned institution is assaulted, destroyed and impoverished, and in which too many characters are divested of their garments.

best in all things. Besides, he didn't feel like moving, far less resisting. But he was nonetheless a little curious.

"How did you know I'd be home?" he asked.

"I didn't," Buckrack replied. "I wasn't looking for you. I needed somewhere to shelter and I remembered your place from the last time we met, when I came and got you out of the hospital then brought you back here. You turning up in the middle of the morning is inconvenient. Now shut up. I need to get something to eat."

Buckrack retreated into the kitchen, and Asterisk began to hear the clatter of utensils. He realised he still had his jacket on, and carefully slipped his hand into various pockets to see if he could find his phone. But Buckrack must have taken it from him. He did find, with a little pulse of joy, the bubble pack of Valium. He popped a tablet out with his thumb and decided, in the circumstances, that two would be preferable, and so snapped out a second. He extricated them and snaffled them surreptitiously between his lips.

There now arose the smell of frying bacon and roasting coffee, the sound of sausages sizzling and eggs spitting. A plate or a cup also seemed to smash on the floor. After about ten minutes Buckrack returned with a small stool and a tray on which there was a large fry-up. He went away again and returned. This time he got down slowly to the floor, grunting, and in a kneeling position eased a cushion under Asterisk's head. He got up again with heavy breaths, and fell onto the seat, parking himself at a table just outside the door where he could watch Asterisk as he ate. The latter observed the American, flipped through 180 degrees, and thought he consumed the food in a slovenly way, like a baby, but slowly, tiredly. Asterisk woozily reflected that this may just be an illusion created by the unusual perspective and the oddity of the situation. Then he fancied he saw a great swelling on the side of Buckrack's head. But he could not make Buckrack's features out too well. It was dim in this corner of the kitchen. It became tiring on his eyes to keep straining to look, and eventually he let them flutter shut.

He began to feel incongruously calm and relaxed. Then he remembered something.

"Why did you call me yesterday?" he asked Buckrack, his eyes still closed.

There was a long silence. He assumed Buckrack was still eating. He forced his eyelids open.

"You called yesterday evening. What did you want?"

The expression on Buckrack's face appeared grave. His quiet now took on the air of a thoughtful hush. He had finished eating. He was looking directly at Asterisk.

"You got put through to my deputy. Told him to tell me you called."

Buckrack continued to stare, immobile.

Asterisk closed his eyes again. He heard himself say snoozily, "Why?" Then he conked out.

As the man on the floor fell into a sleep, Buckrack was gazing at him stonily, a sliver of egg-whitey drool trickling an inch from the corner of his lips, reaching the curve of his chin and dripping pendulously onto the leg of William Stoner's trousers.

It did occur once or twice to McNamara, on the car journey back to the Trump Building, that he should have been making decisions based on the likelihood that the butterfly effect was in operation, especially when the evidence of consequences was so immediately observable and their magnitude not yet exponential. His walloping Buckrack instinctively on the head had created the circumstances in which Buckrack had thwacked Stoner defensively on the head. If this head-bashing (which he was not aware had already been replicated in classic non-linear dynamic fashion by his suspension of Asterisk, which had led just as directly to the latter's domestic nose-biffing at the end of Buckrack's remaining good arm) was stepped up, deterministic-chaos style, it was bound to lead to much more extreme outcomes than a few personal concussions.[22]

But in truth, although his own self-inflicted headache had gone, his thinking was still hangover-jittery. He could not yet decide with any surety what to do about Buckrack. His thoughts refused to gather and cluster around the problem and quarantine it with a likely solution. They kept zinging toward it and bouncing off at tangents. So he procrastinated, in the hope that there may be a particular Muse[23] which eventually descends to aid beleaguered University Vice Chancellors who caused wounded and dangerous ex-CIA officers to run amok on campus and assault their staff.

---

[22] The reader of the trilogy knows, unlike McNamara, that his violent action is not the *primum mobile* he thinks it is: Buckrack at the end of volume one, after all, smashes a whisky bottle over Sir Evan Covet's noddle before stringing him up with aerial wire. The American has a demonstrated predilection for the baton on the cephalon. Given this fact, McNamara's failure to find adequate motivation for clubbing Buckrack and restraining him with flex (other than being randomly drunk and redoubtably schooled in Glaswegian methods for resolving disagreements) is somewhat beside the point. It is, rather, an obvious narratological symmetry, a result of a different kind of determinism, the artistic kind that novelists get to impose upon their characters.

[23] Or a *deus ex machina*, more likely. Just you wait and see.

Jagger Harmwell was waiting, with another besuited man, when he got back to his office.

"This is Phileas Foremost," said Harmwell, doing the honours, "from Security Solutions. I think he has what we need."

McNamara blinked once at the ridiculous literariness of modern names (this one surely had been made up, he dispiritedly reflected),[24] but said nothing.

"How does it work?" he asked briskly, gesturing at the technical box of tricks Foremost was removing from

---

[24] One could compose a small disquisition on the matter of names and the idiosyncratic way they are dealt with in this trilogy of novels. We can be sure that Robert McNamara's is not "made up": like almost everyone in the meeting of persons who considered Jane Blake's Public Interest Disclosure in volume one, his name is inexplicably filched from those of the real Cabinet members of John F. Kennedy's U.S. government. "William Stoner" has similarly leaked into the second and third of these campus novels from an earlier (but opposite of comic) example of the genre by the unsensationally named American author, John Williams. We know that "Cannon Buckrack" is a self-confessed sobriquet in which violence and extortion seem consciously united. "Sir Evan Covet" is little more than an obvious political-party anagram, although it does additionally typify the character's vices in the transparent manner of Renaissance and Restoration comedy (indeed, there is a Lady Covet in Thomas May's *The Old Couple*, a long-forgotten play published posthumously in 1658); "Redman" is likewise a patently ideological charactonym; while "Asterisk", suggesting a mere glyph which acts only to blank out a meaningful character notionally existing underneath it, aptronymically signifies the Registrar's obvious lack of spiritual distinction. Other examples could be copiously cited. On the occasions on which we (and McNamara) meet absurdities like "Phileas Foremost", however, we (and McNamara) may legitimately be thinking that we have simply wandered into a light vernal fog of randomly associative personal designations generated by a lazily time-serving author who is beginning to make even his own protagonist impatient.

a dark vinyl bag.

Foremost seemed rather proud of the machine – which looked exactly like a black-framed Etch A Sketch with a single knob – as if he had invented it himself. "Nothing escapes detection with this. Japanese. Used by Mossad. It's called The Tapfinder. Its range is thirty metres in diameter, so significantly larger than this room. Look, I'll show you."

He took a small button-shaped black flat rectangle from a recess in the back of The Tapfinder.

"This little thing is a typical modern wireless consumer listening device. It has a SIM in it, it and calls the person who put it there, or they can also call it and listen in, in real time. There are more advanced ones which, once switched on, also record and transmit audio data on the fly on a pre-set frequency to whoever wants to listen in to it later. Now, if I put this on the desk, here, and step away a few feet, all I have to do is turn the dial slowly on The Tapfinder, and it scours the entire frequency range throughout the room."

While this was going on, Harmwell looked sidelong at McNamara. "When I come to think of it," he said, "we should maybe have done this long ago, given everything that happened in the first term, though I was told no evidence of bugs had been found."

McNamara did not reply.

The Tapfinder gave a small chirrup of alarm.

"And there we are!" exclaimed Foremost triumphantly. He took a few steps back towards McNamara. "Not only does it detect it, but it shows here on the screen exactly where it is, and how far away on the x and y axes."

He picked up the model listening device, switched it off and replaced it in its plastic cavity.

"Now I'll do two entire passes," Foremost explained, "once up the entire frequency range, and once back down it. If there's anything else in the room it will find it."

McNamara and Harmwell watched and waited.

After forty seconds Foremost looked up and said, "Nothing. No bugs here."

"Good," said McNamara. "Now come with me."

He took them along the corridor to repeat the exercise in Asterisk's office.

It took a mere five seconds for The Tapfinder to locate an eavesdropping device on the undersurface of the desk. Foremost put his index finger to his lips. He crawled into the kneehole of the desk with his phone light on and found it magnetically attached to one of the metal brace plates on the left. He found its power switch and turned it off.

When he brought it out, he put on the top of the desk a small grey box about the width and thickness of a 9-volt battery, which was much larger than the button devices McNamara had found before.

McNamara made to ask a question, but Foremost waved a hand at him to be silent.

Foremost continued to turn the dial on The Tapfinder cautiously. After fifteen seconds or so, when he was close to the top of the frequency range on the first pass, the machine pipped again. Foremost looked at its screen, then glanced askew at McNamara and Harmwell. Then he inclined forward, pulled the top left drawer all the way out, bent over, looked into the drawer slot, put his hand in, fumbled for a moment, and removed an identical small box (but this time black rather than grey). It had been attached with an adhesive pad to the underside of the desktop within the drawer slot.

After completing the upward pass and another downward pass on The Tapfinder with no further result, Foremost said, "We can speak now. I have switched both of them off."

He bent over and looked at two devices. "Oh, wow," he whispered.

"I thought these things were meant to be small and inconspicuous?" McNamara said. "These seem pretty large."

"Yeah, they're not your usual consumer devices. Those tend to be smaller because the assumption is that you have access to them and can replace the battery every now and again. Like this one here in the back of The Tapfinder, they tend to run out of charge after a few days or, with power saving, a couple of weeks at most. It's the kind of thing a husband puts in his home to catch a cheating wife, or to monitor conversations you know are going to happen soon. But not these."

"What do you mean?" said McNamara.

"These are bespoke. The reason they are so relatively large, well, let's see, shall we?"

He opened the battery compartment of both devices. Inside each was a double stack of chunky silver button cells.

"Oh my God," said Foremost.

"What?" said McNamara.

"That," said Foremost, pointing, "is an array of eight LR1154 cells. When one fails, the next kicks in. It's the kind of arrangement you deploy when you want longevity in a small device. One of these cells is commonly used as a CMOS battery in a computer to power the real-time clock and retain BIOS settings, and lasts for years. If you put them in an array like this you can power a small device continuously for, well, months, probably longer as these things pretty much go to sleep until noise activates them. You can put these somewhere and leave them and not have to go back to them."

"You mean it's for, what, continuous long-term surveillance?"

"Yes. I mean, this is ... MI5-level stuff. Also, look, no markings, no serial numbers on the device itself. You can't buy these for thirty quid on Amazon."

The three men stood looking at the two little boxes.

"Is there anything we can do that would tell us where they came from?" Harmwell suggested.

"I doubt it," said Foremost. "Concealment is the objective. The best you could do is test the voltage in the batteries, and that would be a good indication of which was placed earlier and which later. I can do that now. I have a multimeter with me in my car. I mention this because there's something altogether weird about this."

"What's that?" McNamara asked.

"Well," said Foremost, "it's not uncommon to find several bugs in a largish room. This is the obvious place to put one, on the work desk, on the side where the phone is. A lot of talking gets done at an office desk. So you'd expect that. But you'd put the second bug somewhere else, like over there, across the room near that chaise-longue, armchair and coffee table arrangement. You wouldn't place it a few inches away from the first, like these two, would you? You'd simply be duplicating data that way. You see what I'm saying?"

McNamara said, "Please spell it out for me so that I am certain."

"I'm saying it's my guess that two different people

bugged the room," Foremost clarified. "Whoever put the second bug in did not know the first one was already here."

Chapter Nine

McNamara decided it was time to speak to Detective Superintendent Nesbit. He could not find his own card with the CID man's number and asked Meifeng to call Buckinghamshire Police.

At last he felt that he was beginning to piece together what had been happening. Foremost had tested the batteries in the two devices. Six of the eight in the black box were discharged, and three in the grey box. An arithmetical relation between these two facts led him to conclude that both devices were CIA issue. Buckrack had last been seen over six months ago, and had been in Asterisk's office alone, where he had placed the black bug in the Registrar's desk drawer; a CIA officer had interviewed Asterisk in his office three months ago, reached under the desk and placed the grey one on the metal bracing plate. Buckrack had been listening in to Asterisk's conversations since early November, the CIA since late February. This was obviously how Buckrack knew that Asterisk had been visited by Nesbit. And now the CIA presumably knew that their powered-down bug had been discovered.

Meifeng called to tell him that Dr Poon had arrived for their meeting. He put the two listening devices in his desk drawer, staring at them thoughtfully before he closed it. He marvelled at his own lack of any sense of drama. Odium had these days come to seem a place where almost anything was possible. Being bugged by the CIA at the whim of Donald Trump and having to deal with a rogue ex-Agency employee were not experiences he had expected on assuming the role of Vice Chancellor of an English university, but he was beginning to take them in his stride. It made other things – like the thing he was about to do – appear comparatively simple.

Avril Poon entered serious-faced and haughty, with something of a strut, sat down without ceremony, and glared at McNamara across the desk.

"Thank you for coming to see me," he began. "I thought we should talk."

"It would have been nice to have been spoken to, as the Union President, before you issued the letter about the redundancies."

McNamara replied, "It's not actually about the redundancies that I wished to speak with you. The letter that went out today announces the beginning of a consultation to which all the campus unions will, of course, be invited. The information had to be kept confidential until we were sure about the way forward. No, what I wanted to discuss with you is this." He tapped a forefinger on some papers on the surface of his desk. "This is a notice of a private prosecution against the University by the family of Jane Blake," he continued. "It contains an affidavit from you swearing that the University, including me and James Redman as named parties, concealed the existence of a listening device in your office last autumn."

Poon harrumphed. "So what? It's true, isn't it?"

"It's arguable. Our saying nothing in order to protect the University from bad publicity is not necessarily active concealment. Redman and I were also bugged. We weren't under any obligation to comment publicly on the affair. It's true that we agreed not to participate in the internal investigation that sought to confirm if the bugs existed. We did not consider that such a revelation would do the institution any good, to wit the probable planting of those bugs by a student our ex-Vice Chancellor murdered, especially given the stormy waters we were then sailing in, to wit the fact that we were in the middle of a hostile takeover bid by another university. But your affidavit rather glosses over this context, and the fact that it was me who actually *revealed* to you that there was a bug in your office in the first place. Whatever I did, I did not conceal it from *you*. But I was wondering what you hoped to gain from involving yourself as a witness in this prosecution against your employer?"

"To gain?" Poon scoffed. "What makes you think it's about gain? It's about justice."

"Justice?" said McNamara. "Are you sure? Is there no admixture of motives of revenge? Or of wishing to justify your own less than temperate actions?"

"Think what you like."

"Okay, but have you considered also how much you have to lose? I mean, personally? Imagine this case goes to court and you are subject to cross-examination. Jane Blake's accusations about your sexual harassment of her were also concealed from public knowledge for the same reason the existence of the bugs was concealed, so you yourself were spared the indignity of being asked about them by the press. You won't be so well treated in an open trial."

Poon glowered back at him archly. "We've had something like this conversation before. Do your worst. But maybe you now understand why I am cooperating with her family. Sure, I misbehaved. Or rather, as I would put it, I was misled by a beautiful young woman bent on seduction. You may not have noticed that that is common and permissible between women these days. But nothing actually happened. It was just words. I temporarily lost my sense of professional judgment. And now she's dead. I didn't cause her death, but assisting her family is one way of making restitution for my weakness in respect of her. In any case, I'd say the chances of this case going to court are near to zero. You'll settle, if you're wise."

"You are doing this to *atone*?" McNamara said with more than a hint of incredulity. "That would dem-onstrate a nobility of moral conduct which, forgive me, I find it difficult to associate with your person."

"Sneer all you like," Poon replied.

"Okay," McNamara sighed. "I take it, then, that you intend to offer your resignation?"

For the first time Poon looked startled. "Why would I do that?"

McNamara stared back evenly. "Your employer protected your reputation by keeping confidential details of your actions which, surely, in the eyes of public opinion, you must agree, would have damaged it beyond repair. You don't seem minded to reciprocate. You cannot expect your employer to continue to have confidence in you if you participate in a prosecution of them concerning the very same matter. And you patently have no confidence in your employer. It would therefore be logical for you to part company with us at this juncture, no? Or do you expect us to still keep paying your salary while you collaborate in an action against us?"

"You can't fire me over this!" Poon exclaimed. "I'd take you to an employment tribunal and win, and then all the dirty laundry you are trying to conceal would be publicly aired."

"Oh," said McNamara, "I think we could. All an employer has to demonstrate for legal dismissal is their justifiable loss of confidence in the employee, and I think we can persuasively do that. But I didn't say anything about firing you. I said I assumed you would wish to resign if you intend to remain on your present course. We currently have two positions earmarked for redundancy in your department in any case, and your resignation would spare us one."

"What?" Poon lurched forward in disgust. "You're threatening to engineer my redundancy?"

"Oh, Avril," McNamara said, shaking his head, "you of all people know how redundancy works. It's never 'engineered'. It's a professionally conducted consultation. Everyone is looked at carefully, each person is assessed, their relative academic merits and demerits are weighed in the balance, their value and cost to the institution compared. Your predatory sexual advances towards a murdered female student, your demagogic coordination of an illegal strike, your public support for the academic freedom of a student and a junior administrator who were both entirely in the wrong and did not, in any case, enjoy the legally protected rights to academic freedom in the first place, no, these would of course be disregarded. We're much more likely to examine your research record. And what do we have? A book on *Star Trek*, an edited volume on *The Simpsons*, and a forthcoming treatise about fans of TV adaptations of Sherlock Holmes stories? Your work shows a tendency towards exploring, what shall we call it, the very obviously popular? We'd compare it to your colleagues' work. For example, how does it stand up against Professor Crumpington's recently published landmark 600-page history of American documentary film? Of course, we'd consider your relative years of service also, because the longer the service the greater the severance we would have to pay. Professor Crumpington has twenty-two years' service. You have nine."

Poon appeared on the verge of fulminating aloud, but seemed to think twice, and rested back in her seat.

"On the other hand," McNamara proposed, "we don't always calculate these things so crudely. For example, while we disregard matters of misconduct if they have not been subject to formal disciplinary procedures, we would place a high premium on actions which unambiguously show great loyalty to the University. Research profile and money are not the only currencies around here."

Poon stewed for a moment. "You mean," she said, "actions like withdrawing my participation in the Blake family prosecution?"

McNamara gave her a very gentle smile.

"For example," he said.

James Redman had called Drusilla Frost shortly after noon. She was just about to board a train returning from London. Her mother's dementia was getting worse and she had not even recognised her only daughter. Redman updated her on the redundancy situation and she braced herself to deal with the media cascade which would inevitably begin its first trickle later that afternoon. She had taken the day off and told her office to issue no comment in order to postpone the coming ordeal until the following day.

But Redman did not wish to talk only about the redundancies. He wanted to discuss McNamara.

"Does Robert seem himself to you?" he asked.

"I don't know what you mean," Drusilla replied.

"I'm worried about him. His health. I saw him late last night and he collapsed."

"Collapsed?"

"Well, he was pretty drunk, but he seemed, you know, beyond just normal levels of dissipation. Then he went completely comatose."

"I see."

"Then I called him at lunchtime to see how he was. His assistant said he had gone to the hospital."

Redman heard her say that she could not go into it properly right now, but as it sounded serious she would drop by his office straight off the train in a couple of hours.

Now he was waiting for her to arrive from the station when he got a call from McNamara. He was standing in his office. He preferred not to sit because his ungovernable inter-thigh area, in his mental imaginings at least, seemed more cantaloupes than jingle bells. Perhaps it was himself he should be worried about? If things continued in this growing fashion he would soon probably be able to bounce all the way home on his own two permanently attached spacehoppers.

"James," McNamara said, "I'm going to have to take Poon's name off the redundancy list."

"You're joking!" Redman exclaimed. "This is your chance. You shouldn't pass it up. Why would you? What happened?"

"Of course, I share your disappointment," McNamara said. "I'll explain when I have more time. But I need a replacement from her department. I was wondering about that endlessly annoying little Italian *sfigato*, the one who is always boasting about having met George Lucas. What's his name?"

"Oh, you mean Finocchio Piscialetto?"

"That's it. Let's ditch him instead."

"Oh, well. Agreed, but he's not much of a trophy."

"I know. But needs must. Gotta go. Talk to you soon."

Redman did not have a chance to ask how he had got on at the hospital.

Ten minutes later Drusilla arrived, looking stressed and tired from her journey. Redman insisted she sit down while he made her a reviving brew with his De'Longhi Magnifica automatic bean-to-cup coffee maker, which he told her laughingly he considered superior to McNamara's Gaggia Cadorna Plus in both beverage quality and outer styling, despite the fact that his own was about half the price at a mere three hundred pounds.[25]

When Asterisk woke up he found himself a prisoner in his utility room. He got slowly to his feet and tried the door. He must have been dragged or pushed a little further inside so that it could be swung clear of his head and secured with the key permanently lodged in it on the other side. It did not take long, however, before this key was turned and the door opened. Buckrack stood on the threshold, holding Asterisk's phone.

"What's your passcode?" Buckrack asked.

Asterisk told him. Buckrack tried it.

[25] A duel *ex machina*?

"You got a charging cable?" the American demanded.

"Yes, it should be on the kitchen top near the cooker."

Buckrack looked over his shoulder. "Okay," he said, "let's get moving. Pack an overnight bag. We're going for a drive."

Fifteen minutes later Buckrack, after inspecting with thoroughness the items Asterisk had put into a small valise, with the keys to Asterisk's car in his hand, told him to get into the driver's seat. He went to the boot and put the suitcase in it, then circled round to the passenger door and eased himself in. He handed Asterisk the keys.

"Open the garage door and start the car when I tell you," Buckrack said. "I'll direct you. But first, note this."

So saying, he flashed a six-inch kitchen knife in his hand, which Asterisk recognised as one of his own, whose sharp pointed end he placed a few inches from Asterisk's waist.

"Don't try to fuck around or do anything brave while you are on the road," Buckrack warned. "If you do the slightest thing wrong I'll get you to pull over and throw you in the trunk and drive myself. Keep to the speed limit. Don't contemplate any funny business around a police car. I will use this knife if I have to."

Asterisk gave as harmless a sidelong look as he could muster and nodded. It was only now that he was sitting in proximity to the American that he could smell soap and shampoo. Buckrack had had a shower and cleaned himself up. But he hadn't been able to disguise the ugly bruising and swelling on the side of his head.

"What happened to you?" Asterisk asked. "Did you have an accident?"

"Shut up," said Buckrack. "Now, before we set off,

tell me a bit more about this phone call I was meant to have made to you yesterday. When was that?"

"It was apparently around 6pm. It got put through to my Deputy Registrar because I wasn't there."

"Your Deputy?" What's his name?"

"Elfyn Dethbridge."

Buckrack examined him closely. "Elfyn Dethbridge? What the fuck kind of a name is that?[26] His name has the word death in it?"

Asterisk spelled it out. "D-E-T-H. He's Welsh. In fact, there is a Scottish name spelled D-E-A-T-H, but it's pronounced –"

"Cut the small talk. I'm not interested. What did he tell you about this call?"

"He said it came through to him and when you realised you weren't talking to me you just left a message to tell me you had called. That's all."

"What's he like, this guy, Dethbridge? How long has he worked for you?"

"Well, gosh, he's been my Deputy for about five years. I don't know him too well. We don't socialise."

"You trust him?"

"I'm not sure," Asterisk said with deliberation, "that I trust anyone around here these days. Not after everything that's happened."

---

[26] Even Buckrack is getting impatient about the unlikely names of his fellow characters, despite having chosen an utterly outlandish one for himself. As a matter of fact, however, Welsh boys are called "Elfyn" to this day, and although "Dethbridge" is now rare, modern variants of it (which were mainly deliberate distortions aimed at disguising the mordant sound of its first syllable) include "Deedridge", a name hardly ever found outside of Glamorgan.

"Would he lie?"

"Elfyn?" Asterisk considered. "Oh yes, he would lie. But then, everyone in university senior management lies all the time."

"Does he like you?"

Again, Asterisk pondered for a few seconds and answered, "I doubt it."

"So he'd happily do you harm?"

Asterisk's head bobbed from side to side. "I expect so."

Buckrack looked thoughtful for a couple of moments. At last he said, "Okay. Drive."

As they reversed out of the garage Buckrack plugged Asterisk's phone into the USB charging socket on the dashboard.

"I'm gonna send your boss a text," he told Asterisk. "When he calls back I'll tell you to pull off the road. Now head for the freeway and drive south."

Asterisk's eyes flickered nervously. He did not say it, but he considered Buckrack his boss right now and was going to do whatever he said.

McNamara soon got a call back from Detective Superintendent Nesbit, who started the conversation by congratulating him on stepping into a dead man's gap.

"I heard it on the news," Nesbit said. "Someone should base a soap opera on your university. I mean, you couldn't make it up, could you? Usually all you get is universities boasting to the public about their marvellous achievements. With Odium you get the craziest stuff you normally only see on Netflix. Murder and suicide, terrorist suspects, a showdown with the American President. What next, I wonder?"

"Nothing, I hope," said McNamara. "I was simply calling about your request to view our purchasing records."

"Purchasing records?" he heard Nesbit say quizzically. "My request?"

"Yes, you know, yesterday."

"Yesterday?"

"When you spoke to our Registrar."

"I spoke to your Registrar?"

McNamara began to feel uneasy at Nesbit's echo questions, so asked one of his own.

"You didn't speak to our Registrar yesterday?"

"Did I? Not that I recall. I'm getting old, but I do tend to remember what happened yesterday. Has someone been impersonating me? That's a serious offence, you know. You can get six months for that. Police Act, 1996."

This was said in a chipper, humorous tone. Nesbit clearly thought there had been nothing more than a mix-up.

"Oh," said McNamara. "Obviously there must be some crossed wires at our end. I do apologise."

"Oh, that's alright," said Nesbit. "It happens."

"So, can I ask, since we are speaking, you're not still looking into the Jane Blake murder? It's just that I noticed my predecessor had received the police report a few months back, and I thought I might get asked questions about it by the University Council."

"Oh, no, case closed," said Nesbit.

"And the money that disappeared from her American bank account?"

"Ah, well, that, now that's a loose end which annoyed us for a while, but what can I say? The Americans didn't play ball when we asked for more information. Not that it's so important, mind you. We're pretty confident about our conclusion. Murder followed by suicide of the murderer. Happens all the time in our business."

After the call was over McNamara ate a sandwich he had brought back from the hospital, and cogitated. He found himself oddly enjoying his attempts to put the enigmatic pieces of this new puzzle together, and noticed that nearly all traces of his hangover, other than a besetting weariness, had now disappeared.

Buckrack had bugged Asterisk's office. He had heard Asterisk speaking with someone claiming to be Nesbit. This had alarmed him and prompted him to act. But that person had not been Nesbit. Now, who would have the daring to impersonate a CID officer, and for what purpose?

His thoughts were interrupted by a text from Asterisk. It read, simply, "I have news about Buckrack."

When McNamara called back on his own mobile, Buckrack ignored it. They had just joined the motorway a few miles before, and he instructed Asterisk to take the next exit ramp. He scanned the surroundings and indicated a service area with a large empty car park. When Asterisk parked up, far from any building or other vehicle, he took the keys from him and told him to stay in the car with the windows closed. He stepped out, locked the doors, put the knife in his pocket with his good hand around it, and walked some yards away on the driver's side of the car where he could keep an eye on Asterisk. He noted with some despair that he was still seeing everything in monochrome. Fumbling a little with the phone in his weaker hand, he returned McNamara's call and heard him say, "Hello, Nigel."

"No, it's me, asshole," Buckrack hissed. "Now just fucking listen. First of all, I have Asterisk. If you do anything to try to track me down, I'll kill him. If you don't do what I need you to do, I'll kill him. If you involve the police, I'll kill him."

He heard the long pause as McNamara's brain-clockwork presumably whirred and managed to get its cogs entoothed in this new machinery.

"Let me speak to him," McNamara said.

"Hold on," said Buckrack.

He walked to the car and gestured for Asterisk to open the driver's window.

"You're on speaker. Nothing about location," Buckrack instructed.

"Hello?" McNamara said. "Nigel?"

"Yes, Vice Chancellor," said Asterisk.

"You okay?"

"Yes, Vice Chancellor."

"Are you hurt?"

"Not really."

"Okay. Just cooperate with him. Do as he says. I'll talk to him and sort this out."

"Yes, Vice Chancellor. Thank you."

"That's enough," Buckrack interrupted and took the phone away. He walked some distance away once more. Then he asked, "Why the fuck did you club me on the head and tie me up in your basement?"

To his surprise, he heard McNamara scoff in a manner suggestive of someone who considered that he had the upper hand. "No, you listen to me, *asshole*. You can keep on doing your batshit crazy stuff like you're doing now but you're obviously desperate. If all you wanted was to avoid being associated with a minor bugging scandal you wouldn't go to the extreme of keeping people under surveillance and blackmailing them. You've got much bigger secrets to hide. And while we're about it, apart from now kidnapping one of my senior staff, whose safety I am naturally concerned about, why did you assault and rob another and hospitalise him this morning? And why did you steal his trousers and leave him half naked?"

"That wasn't intentional. But I needed money for a cab. I needed his pants because my own were torn and bloody."

"You hit him with a rock! You knocked him out cold. You could have killed him."

"He came upon me while I was asleep. It was an instant reaction. In any case, I was only there because you fucking decked me. And who the fuck was in my house in the middle of the night? Who did you call? Was that the cops?"

"I didn't call anybody. What are you talking about?"

"When I got to my house there was someone inside with a flashlight. That's why I couldn't go in."

"I fell asleep. I haven't told anyone about you. Not yet."

"Are you for real? I don't know whether to believe you or not."

There was a soft, slow laugh from McNamara down the line. "*You* don't know whether or not to believe *me*? Listen to Mr Sincerity."

"That's why I need some leverage in the form of your guy Asterisk."

"Christ," said McNamara. "All you've done is dig a hole deeper. But I'll tell you what. You want to hear of recent developments that'll make you realise how wrong you are?"

"What developments?"

"Okay, for one, I found your bug in Asterisk's office. It's now in my desk drawer. Your little black box. But

153

you know what? There was a second one, very similar, only grey. Now I'm guessing you didn't put that one there, right? And if that's true, it's obvious who did. And they put it there after yours."

It was Buckrack's turn to pause and process. He stood blinking in the car park. He glanced over at the car and saw Asterisk with his head on the steering wheel. "Let me get this right," he said. "The second box was identical?"

"Pretty much," said McNamara. "So it was CIA, right?"

Buckrack did not answer.

McNamara went on. "And here's another funny thing. The police did not visit Asterisk yesterday morning. Whoever it was, it wasn't Detective Superintendent Nesbit of Buckinghamshire CID."

"How do you know?"

"Because I just called Detective Superintendent Nesbit of Buckinghamshire CID. He was never looking further into the case. As far as he's concerned it's practically closed."

"Fuck! You did call the cops. Did you tell him about me?"

"No. As I said, I've told no one about you. He's never shown the slightest interest in you. I don't think he knows you even exist. But someone does. So let me tell you what I think has happened here and you tell me if I'm wrong. How about that?"

Buckrack grunted, "Go on."

"Alright," said McNamara. "Obviously you got wind of the fact that Asterisk had been questioned by the CIA about you. After all, you had bugged his office in November before you left to keep tabs on his conversations. This is why you came back to Europe

154

and started to watch those who had been involved in your original bugging, the ones you did for Covet, in other words people like me. But it wasn't the bugging that bothered you, rather the fact that you had done much worse things – the money, for one, maybe more – that you had to conceal. As it turned out, Asterisk played dumb about you when the CIA visited him in his office, but unknowns to him they also placed a bug there, because they knew he knew something and they were hoping to find out what it was. But it was you they were interested in. Agent gone rogue kind of thing, is it? Need to get a hold of this criminal ex-CIA guy before what he's done blows up all in public and causes major international embarrassment? I'm speculating. Quite how they realised you were the problem you are I don't know, but I am guessing it's something to do with that transfer of money to the Cayman Islands the British police asked but never got an answer about. Still, they – your old friends at the CIA – needed some concrete evidence of your involvement with Jane Blake and Covet. Obviously they weren't getting this evidence from their bug in Asterisk's office, so they tried to stimulate the situation by sending some guy in to Asterisk yesterday morning, pretending to be Detective Superintendent Nesbit of Buckinghamshire CID, hoping to scare him after they had left into babbling about you in connection with the bugs – and they succeeded. He told Redman about you and they heard him do so. But you, clever guy you, unknowns to anyone at all, even to them, you had your *own* bug in Asterisk's office and heard all of it too, or thought you did. But what you were hearing was that the British police were looking further into the case. You fell for their trick too, even though it wasn't intended for you. And that's what brought you instantly out of whatever woodwork you were hiding in, to me, threatening to blackmail me in order to close down something that, it turns out, wasn't even happening. You didn't just get banged on the head. You got scammed into exposing yourself. Now they know you're here, somehow: you would know how. So, shall we take an informed guess who was in your house with a torch last night, looking for you?"

Buckrack did not reply but his breathing was heavy.

"It really is quite a plot," McNamara continued. "If I saw this in a movie I'd be scoffing with incredulity, myself. Unless it was a spy movie, of course, in which case this would all seem a little underwhelming and petty and simply not thrilling enough."[27]

At last Buckrack exploded, "Damn it!"

"Yeah," McNamara assented laconically. "The only thing I can't figure out is why you called Asterisk last night before you saw me. What were you trying to do, scare him?"

---

[27] McNamara has clearly not twigged that he is in fact trapped in the genre of anti-climactic farce. Clockman presumably does not entitle his closing volume Carry On le Carré (which would approximately sum up its content) because readers these days increasingly do not know what the Carry On movies were all about, or le Carré's espionage novels for that matter (most of them written in the inspiration-destroying knowledge that ponderous and overrated movies or TV mini-series would be based on their ponderous and overrated content). Admittedly it is difficult to envisage Sid James as McNamara or Jim Dale as Redman, though a blacked-up Barbara Windsor as Poon or a Welsh-inflected Charles Hawtrey as Dethbridge are not entirely beyond a wild imagination. One can, however, now easily agree with McNamara's intuitive hint that Buckrack's revealed incompetence would entirely justify calling this novel The Spy Who Crept Out of the Mould.

Buckrack answered, "I didn't. It was them."

"Them?"

"The Agency. It's an old baiting tactic. They wanted to frighten Asterisk into blabbering or acting on impulse. They can't get me to call the guy they want to frighten. So they call someone else and pretend to be me and get that someone else to tell him it was me and so he gets frightened because he's scared of me. Check the phone logs. I bet they didn't call Asterisk at all. I bet they called the other guy direct. What was his name, Deadhead?"

"Dethbridge."

"Yeah, him."

McNamara started in his seat. "Wait a minute!" he exclaimed. "You mean they might be using Dethbridge as some kind of misleading information channel?"

"Exactly."

"But he also appeared here today with a lawsuit."

"A lawsuit?"

"Well, a legal claim for damages. Jane Blake's mother is suing the University."

"She hasn't got a mother. Her mother is dead. There's no mother."

"Alison Blake. Here's her U.S. address and everything. The papers are from a London law firm."

"Her mother was called Alison Blake but that's bullshit. Alison Blake died in a car accident when Jane Blake was a child. You're being played. It's another piece of bait."

"I don't understand."

"Christ, you haven't got it yet? They want *me*. This stuff is done to rattle you and Asterisk into giving me up to them, getting you to help them locate me. All of it, the pretend cop, the call to Dethbridge, the lawsuit – all of them are ploys. None of them are real. They are all deceptions."

"Are you saying there's no lawsuit?"

McNamara heard Buckrack sigh. "It will all look official. There will be a real London law firm and it will have lodged real court papers. They'll have forged documents purporting to prove that Alison Blake is alive. But when you contact them to discuss the case it will be a CIA agent who visits you and they'll be seeking information about me and if you give it they'll promise to make the lawsuit go away. They may even have co-opted Dethbridge to do their work for them. Using him once might be an accident. Using him twice sounds like he's in on it."

"What? How would they do that?"

Buckrack scoffed. "How do you think? Blackmail. Bribery. Is this guy Dethbridge a saint? Does he have reason to dislike you or Asterisk? Does he have something to gain? As I say, check the phone logs. Was there really a call to him or Asterisk last night? Either way, he's bringing you chickenshit. Call the lawyer and see what happens. Call them today and set up a meeting as soon as possible and watch how quickly they come running. The person they send will be an Agency operative. They might have legal qualifications but that won't be their function."

"I see," said McNamara. "I'll do that. And so now you've kidnapped Asterisk as your insurance policy, is that it? You think I won't give you away as long as you've got him? How do you know they're not all up on his phone or mine too and listening in right now?"

"I doubt it. If they were on your phone in real time they would have known I was at your house last night instead of trying to find me at mine. There are methods of capturing phone data but since Edward Snowden the Agency pretty much has to go through GCHQ to get British call information, and they don't want the British to know about me. They want to seize me and get me out without the British being aware. As for Asterisk's phone, I'll be disposing of it after this call and buying a different one to contact you on, and that'll be just text messages from a spoofing service and you won't be able to locate the source. We've already left Odium. Expect no more voice calls."

"And what do you want?"

"It's simple," Buckrack said. "I need your help to get away. You give me that, Asterisk will be fine. You give any sign of cooperating with them or calling in the police, he won't be. I'm figuring you might not care too much personally about Asterisk, and you don't seem too susceptible to personal blackmail. But I think you might just not be prepared to let him die. So all you have to do is stall at your end. I need time. One of the reasons I need time is that you fucking brained me and I am injured and I need two or three days to recover and make a plan. So just do nothing. It's really that simple. Can we agree to that?"

McNamara said, "But I'll need to be able to speak to Asterisk frequently to check that he's okay."

"That's not going to happen," Buckrack replied. "But I may send you the odd photo as proof. You call that lawyer and I'll text you later this evening."

"Okay," said McNamara, becoming habituated now to the relentless skulduggery. Then a suitably cunning thought occurred to him. "By the way, do you still have access to what your listening device picks up if I turn it on again?"

"I do," said Buckrack.

Chapter Ten

At around this time, Redman was withdrawing his post-climax penis from Drusilla Frost's still quivering vagina.

Their afternoon had seemingly proceeded seamlessly (but not semenlessy or without steaminess and seaminess and lubricating creaminess) from conversation to consolation to concern to conviviality to condominium to concoctions to concupiscence to condom to congress, but their consummation was not about to be consolidated by consanguinity; rather (on one side at least) it was to result in concealed conscientious contrition.

In other words, they had talked; Drusilla had expressed her sadness at her mother's worsening dementia; she had appeared worried by what Redman had to say about McNamara's possibly terminal condition and his sudden visit to the hospital at lunch time; they had indulged in the alleviation of mental distress which tends to be dispensed by gallows humour; Drusilla said she really wanted a drink and Redman had suggested going back to his place; he had mixed them some early cocktails; mutual lust was now strong enough to be acknowledged actively; a prophylactic was unspokenly considered advisable for obvious reasons even if pregnancy was out of the question; they fucked; both of them had orgasms, Drusilla first (and for the first time ever); she ostensibly found it all exhilarating; he, after enjoying the long-wished-for relief it afforded, rapidly became horrified at their impulsive perfidy, and did his best to hide it.

As he lay back on his pillow and felt his post-coital testes re-assume the comfortable size and consistency of pitted olives, he was aware of Drusilla's face hovering beside him, bearing a lascivious, shameless, satisfied smirk. He could not reciprocate it fully so gave back a tight little smile and tried to calculate how long he would have to spend in reassuring after-talk before he could put some distance between himself and what he had failed to consider beforehand: Drusilla's flabby breasts, greying hair, cellulitic buttocks and limited intelligence, as well as the now once more impinging facts of her being the partner of his long-time friend and possibly dying boss and of having personally detested her for nearly all the years he had known her.

Drusilla, on the other hand, did not appear to be afflicted with parallel neurotic seizures. She had clearly enjoyed the athletic pounding she had received, and all the edges of her previous anxiety seemed to have been blurred into comfort by it. She stretched languidly for five minutes and gave the impression of being at ease in her naked body. Nor did she seem too bothered by a need to talk. She made some dreamily intoned, flattering remark about the powers of a younger man; said that she'd have liked another drink but had better not, as she had to drive home; got up and got dressed; but left him in no doubt, as she let herself out, still simpering with deliberate archness as she left his bedroom, that she was looking forward to more sometime soon. Redman could only hope privately that when she saw McNamara again she would reconsider.

He mooned around his house for an hour. He tried to drink another cocktail but this only intensified his guilt and his sense of being the careless one in a classic mess-of-pottage scenario. He went for a shower but discovered that no matter how much he scrubbed himself he was also now trapped in a dismayingly clichéd all-the-perfumes-of-Arabia situation.[28] When the thought came into his mind that going for a run might help him flee his despair, he abandoned the idea almost immediately in the knowledge now that which way he fled was hell, his self was hell, and in the lowest deep a lower deep, still threatening to devour him, opened wide, to which the hell he suffered now would seem a heaven.

Dethbridge was still enjoying the feeling of settling into Asterisk's office when McNamara arrived unann-ounced. The Vice Chancellor seemed to be unusually breezy, certainly much more pleasant in manner than Dethbridge had ever experienced before. He was carrying the envelope that Dethbridge had handed him earlier that day.

"So, this lawsuit which was delivered to you this morning," McNamara said. "I'd like you to deal with it.

---

[28] Lady Macbeth has, paradoxically, reduced Redman to a haunted conscience. This and the blatant Miltonic allusion in the following sentence would seem to provide the warning that everyone should be given before they choose to study it – that knowledge of English Literature serves mainly to rub aggravating salt into the moral wounds of those who acquire it.

Call the lawyer and ask for a meeting here in person, would you? Make the call today before close of business. Tell them you'd like to see them at their earliest convenience. Say nothing about my having read it. In fact, give them to understand that you have not even passed it on but that you'd like to have a preliminary discussion with them about it."

"Er, really?" Dethbridge said. "But why? I am not sure I understand. What would I say at a meeting with them? I can't imagine you would wish me to speak for the University on this matter, surely?"

"Oh no, of course not. I just want you to listen to what they have to say and then let me know while they are here. Depending on what they say, I may also meet with them. Just keep it simple. Call them, request a meeting here as soon as possible, and let me know when it is. And, as I say, do it now. I suspect they will want to meet pretty soon."

Dethbridge nodded obediently despite his puzzlement, and McNamara left.

He took out his mobile phone and tapped twice on its screen. He heard the soft feminine intonations of his American blackmailer as she answered.[29]

---

[29] But, ah, the cunning power of literature to deceive! Until almost this point in the narrative we have been misled into assuming, have we not, that Dethbridge's blackmailer was first of all Buckrack himself but, even after that illusion was potentially dispelled, that the minatory voice at the end of the phone belonged to a man? Now it is suddenly revealed (in a manner simple to contrive in a novel but very difficult to pull off in a movie) that this previously coarse-talking CIA arm-twister is in fact a dulcetly enunciating woman. Shame on us for our sexist prejudices. What next? Are we to discover that J. D. Clock*man* is a deliberately deceptive name also?

"So," she said, "You have news for me?"

"Yes," said Dethbridge cautiously.

"Where are you?" she asked.

"I'm in Asterisk's office."

"You are? And Asterisk?"

"He's, well ... gone. Off sick, apparently, and will be for some time."

"I see. And what else?"

"I gave him the document a couple of hours ago. He came back to me and said he wants me to organise a meeting."

"As expected."

"But no. He wants a meeting between me and you, not you and him. He told me to give you the impression that he hadn't seen the document, like it was simply me calling you in response to receiving it."

"Right," came the reply. "Well, you go back and tell him no. Say we'll be happy to meet with him, but with no one else."

"I can do that," Dethbridge said. "But why do you think he wanted me to pretend?"

"Don't ask questions," said his interlocutor, and then she hung up.

Dethbridge picked up the desk phone, called internally to McNamara and relayed to him the bare bones of this conversation. McNamara told him to call the lawyer back and make an appointment for her to meet as she requested with him as soon as possible. Much to McNamara's surprise, Dethbridge called him back a few moments later and said that the lawyer was prepared to meet with him later this evening at, say, around 9pm? This sounded satisfyingly unusual to McNamara: what real lawyer would travel from London at the drop of a hat outside normal business hours when the appointment was not urgent and could easily be made for the morning after? Buckrack had been right. The "lawyer" was probably not in London at all, but already in Odium. The delay of several hours in the proposed meeting was most likely a contrivance to make it appear that a journey was necessary. The suggestion, however, also fitted with McNamara's own sense of urgency.

He looked at his watch. It was now 4.25pm. He called Dethbridge back and told him to instruct the lawyer to report to the security office when she arrived, where she would be escorted to their meeting.

Asterisk had spent an uncomfortable two hours at the wheel. He did not know where they were going and kept obsessively guessing as they passed junction after junction on the M1, until Buckrack instructed him laconically to travel east at Milton Keynes. His Valium had worn off and he was becoming more anxious, and with good reason. All the while there was the tip of Buckrack's sharp blade in the rolls of fat that cascaded over the waistband of his trousers. He drove cautiously to the side of road bumps and slowed down at approaching small waves and troughs in the otherwise monotonous motorway surface (of which he was becoming hypersensitively aware), but even so, still he felt the near-piercing pinch of the point of the poignard become more intercostally acute every so often. It took him a while to work out that this was because Buckrack was, every few minutes, involuntarily twitching. Occasionally he was able to steal a furtive sideways glance at his kidnapper and see with mounting alarm that white saliva was slowly oozing from the corner of his mouth where his missing canine tooth had been, and sliding greyly down his chin and dripping off, unnoticed, onto the front of his shirt.

"There should be a pack of tissues in the glove compartment," Asterisk said once, hoping to ingratiate himself.

"What?" Buckrack replied, with what seemed like absent-mindedness.

"Your chin," Asterisk gestured.

Buckrack put his left hand up to his face. He did not feel any wetness because his fingers were tingling and numb, but he saw it blurrily on their tips when he withdrew them. After an over-lengthy pause he became unpredictably concerned of a sudden with comparative dialects. "Glovebox. It's called a glove*box*." He clumsily pulled at the small door (which he did not close but left open for the rest of the journey) and fished out a pack of Handy Andies.

Asterisk could observe fitfully only the phenomenal consequences of an act of which he was not aware, namely McNamara's dual hammer blow to Buckrack's cranium. The reason Buckrack was having difficulty saying things off the top of his head was that there no longer was a top to his head: the summit of his pate was visibly depressed like a sandhill after a moderate subsidence in its centre; the side of his skull around the ear was radically stoved in and brownly-blackly-redly-yellowly stained, the material displaced from the crater having rearranged itself in an alarming bulge that now swelled forward across his right temple, even pushing his brow out on that side so that a protuberant ledge had now formed over his right eye.

Fiction, fortunately, allows us to enter the heads of our characters more fully. McNamara's first blow had, in fact, not merely concussed Buckrack, but fractured

166

the skull at the coronal suture, the joint of tissue on either side of which the frontal bone and parietal bones align. The damage had gone as deep as the upper cerebrum, and caused significant damage to both the somatomotor and somatosensory cortices. His optic nerve had been none too happy at this vandalism in its neighbourhood, which was the reason it had gone on work-to-rule, as it were, and imposed a state of achromatopsia. The canalicular segment of his facial nerve on the right side had joined it in sympathy after being mildly mangled by the second strike, which had caused a large dent around the frontal angle of the parietal bone. This was the cause of the buzzing tinnitus in his right ear but, more seriously, the seemingly craniosynostotic effect which had resulted on the front right of the head was having slowly repercussive consequences across virtually all aspects of his brain geography. Imagine the mainland of Britain being thrust into the coasts of France, Belgium and Holland: the effects will be felt in Bulgaria. And so it was that, even on the unmolested left hemisphere, the posterior inferior frontal gyrus had begun to act up under the pressure, as Asterisk was soon to witness in Buckrack's increasingly evident misperformances in speech.

Not that there was much speech in the remainder of the trip. Buckrack guided mainly by cursory gestures with his stiff left hand accompanied by nasal grunting. Eventually they trundled into a small village, travelled its length, went past a weeping-willowy pond with two islets, turned right, then left into a gravel drive with a FOR SALE sign, and pulled up before a double garage next to a charming cottage in ample, isolated grounds.

"Oh my God," said Asterisk, at last recognising the place. "Why here?"

"Gimme keys," said Buckrack, ignoring his question. "Grout."

"I beg your pardon?" said Asterisk, offering the keys but not understanding the last syllable.

"Out!" spat Buckrack, waving the knife.

Asterisk exited the car and stood looking at the building. In the early summer heat the front lawn had become markedly overgrown.

"But what on earth are we doing here?" Asterisk protested.

Buckrack was impatient. "Grin!"

"I'm sorry?"

Buckrack grasped him by the arm and pulled him. "In!"

They approached a blue front door. Buckrack fumbled in his pocket and produced a set of keys, which he failed to apply accurately to the lock and dropped. He made to bend over to pick them up but the blood rushing painfully to his head dissuaded him and he quickly rose upright again. He pointed at the keys on the gravel. "Grem!"

"Get them?" Asterisk guessed.

Buckrack nodded minimally. Asterisk bent down and retrieved the keys, holding them up before the door. "Shall I?" he offered.

Buckrack motioned his assent and Asterisk unlocked the door. He turned and handed the keys back to Buckrack. "I hope you don't mind me asking, but how is it that you have keys to Sir Evan Covet's home?"

Buckrack did not answer but pushed him in a bundling manner through the opened door. Knowing the house well from his several visits to it, and the new-buyer-inhibiting fact that he had murdered two people in it only six months' before, he quickly located the

168

windowless cellar, half-shepherded, half-intimidated Asterisk into it, and made the door fast behind him. A few minutes later he located a bucket and some toilet roll upstairs, opened the cellar door again, and brought the two items limpingly down the steps, still holding the knife in one hand. He put the bucket down and took a debit card from Asterisk's wallet, which he had earlier confiscated, and now extricated from a shirt pocket.

"PIN nummah," he said.

"I beg your pardon?" said Asterisk, looking with grim disappointment at the bucket.

"Gimme."

Asterisk had by now, curiously, got used to the idea that his life was in danger, but not his bank balance. "I say," he protested meekly, "are you going to steal from me too?" He suddenly wanted to Google to discover whether or not kidnap victims might be eligible for court compensation and was aggrieved that Buckrack had destroyed his phone. This line of thought was cut short as Buckrack raised the knife and displayed a manic expression on his now decidedly asymmetrical face. Asterisk uttered the PIN number aloud.

As Buckrack retreated up the steps, Asterisk heard him say, "Bringya foo soo." He translated this in his head and reflected that he was, indeed, rather hungry.

McNamara asked Meifeng to order the phone logs for the last two days on Asterisk's and Dethbridge's lines. Like almost all Vice Chancellorial requests, this one was met with the toadying rapidity with which his subjects supply an emperor's expressed needs. Meifeng received the logs from the communications centre by email within fifteen minutes, printed them out and brought them to McNamara in his office.

There had been no phone calls to Asterisk's or Dethbridge's university phones after 5pm on the previous day, as Dethbridge had claimed. Moreover, the only calls Dethbridge had made from Asterisk's office that afternoon were the ones he had made internally to McNamara about the meeting with the lawyer. The three calls he must have made to the lawyer were not logged, which could only mean that he had made them on his own mobile, and why would he do that? Once more, McNamara was forced to acknowledge to himself that Buckrack seemed to have assembled the puzzling pieces of the jigsaw accurately. Having put Buckrack's bug back into Asterisk's office before Dethbridge appropriated it, he hoped for further confirmation after Buckrack listened to the exchanges.

At 5pm he went home, where he found Drusilla, slightly tipsy and seemingly very happy, with a drink already in her hand, watching TV. She said that she had sent Chivers home and was planning (a rare occurrence) to make dinner for them both.

"How was your mother?" he asked, embracing her and kissing her on the cheek.

"Much the same," she replied.

"When did you get back?"

"A couple of hours ago," she said. "What has your day been like? I see the redundancy email went out."

"You'll have a busy day with the press tomorrow."

"Well, that's tomorrow," she said breezily. "For tonight, let's kick back and relax."

"I can't," he said. "Well, not in the gin and tonic way you mean. I drank too much last night. I have to go back in for a meeting at nine. I'm going to try to snatch some sleep before then. It's been an exhausting day. I'll forego dinner. Leave me some for later."

Drusilla did not object. Her mind was rather more enamoured with the warm sexual glow which persisted in her flesh than in conversing with the known (and now rather negligible) quantity which was Robert McNamara. This warmth was so insulating that it slipped her mind to probe him about the possibility that he had terminal cancer.

It was when Buckrack took the wheel of Asterisk's car to drive into Aylesbury (having taken a flat cap he found in the bottom of Covet's wardrobe which partly concealed his head wounds) that the extent of his visual problems truly struck home. The colourimetrics of his eyesight could not now have been measured in the 256 greyscale intensities of even a standard computer monitor. It was nowhere near as good as watching a black-and-white movie. It was much more degraded than that. It was not simply the colour-detecting cones of his retina which had been affected, but the light and shade-discerning rods as well. His vision was now capable only of something that fell roughly between the qualities of 2-bit and 4-bit greyscale, allowing him to make out perhaps eight shades, often stained or mottled, with no extremes of pure white (the brightest things were a murky cream) or deep black (the darkest appeared as a smoky, onyx-like grey). He now saw in distinct geometric chunks rather than in a smooth continuum, and when in serious motion, like in charge of a vehicle, this sensory deficit proved to be quite terrifying. It meant navigating a suburban architecture rendered Cubist and drained of nearly all tint.

Traffic lights were not the worst problem, although they were a significant one. He was relieved when he was able to trundle up behind a car already stationary at them and simply follow its lead, for otherwise he had no means of discerning when the lights changed. On the two occasions he found himself the lead car at a red light he waited until someone behind hooted for him to move on its turning green. But there were greater hazards. When luminosity abruptly altered, as when he drove under an overpass and was plunged into artificial darkness, he was incapable of seeing anything at all in the black void immediately before him, and then when he hit the large canvas of beckoning daylight beyond, everything became blindingly, contrastingly over-exposed and washed out for a second or two. Shadows of trees and telegraph poles cast over the road at first made him think he was about to clatter disastrously into an earthquaky, Californian fissure in the surface of the world that had instantaneously cracked open before him, and took getting used to. As he pootled through the outskirts like a paranoiac pensioner, his peripheral perception was too poor to notice other drivers casting sidelong, judgmental stares at him. Luckily he found a retail park off the main road into town, and stationed the car as close to the outlets as he could.[30]

[30] This must be the Vale Hundreds Retail Park, just off the A418 at Aylesbury, which I can confirm in May 2017 possessed a mobile phone outlet called Matrix Communications, an Aldi supermarket, and a sizeable B&Q DIY centre. The description of his journey suggests that Buckrack drove towards the town on this same road. Given that his trip, though an existential challenge, was not of long duration, one is tempted to guess that the village in which Covet's cottage is located is Aston Abbotts, approximately four miles to the north of Aylesbury, not least because it has the requisite twin-islanded pond of the hamlet's earlier description (at the south-ernmost bend of Moat Lane).

The first thing he bought was a cheap mobile phone from a small electrical store, using Asterisk's name, address and debit card. Asterisk had not lied about the PIN number. Buckrack was even pathetically gratified that he could still manage to decipher digits and writing, but he became aware that interactions with others now seemed excruciatingly, inordinately laborious and anxiety-inducing. He could understand what the woman behind the counter was saying to him in her unusual accent, but it sounded like an interminable drone, and he negotiated her seemingly endless, upbeat questions and comments largely by means of repeated nods, grunts and affirmative ums, expecting that in disability-aware England she would simply assume, with personable charity, that he had learning difficulties or some such (which he technically now did). Then he went into a nearby supermarket and threw some ready-made sandwiches into a basket and got out as quickly as he could. Finally, he entered a DIY superstore, which was what he had really been looking for. He perambulated around it with a large trolley for twenty minutes and emerged with the following items:

> two heavy fibre glass panels, about two feet by three feet, of the kind used for internal dropped ceilings;

> twelve sturdy kitchen knives, all of the same type and length, with a one-foot blade and a four-inch handle;

> twelve packets of builder's putty, each about three inches square, sealed in plastic;

> a fifty-metre length of blue (though it looked grey to him) three-strand polypropylene rope, eight millimetres in thickness;

a pair of heavy-duty scissors;

a roll of duct tape;

a hammer;

a packet of nails;

a six-pack of ultra-thin rubber gloves;

a bag of hooks of the kind used to secure curtain tiebacks.

These he tipped into the boot of the car before making the nervous but eventless drive back to Covet's cottage. He had been gone just over an hour. It was 4.45pm. He wasted no time in unloading his purchases and spreading them on the living room floor, with the exception of the sandwiches. These he threw without ceremony down into the basement for Asterisk to eat. He had no appetite himself. While he waited for the phone SIM to become network-active (the woman in the store had told him this should happen quite rapidly), he occupied himself with constructing the two simple homemade contraptions he had envisaged in his mind's eye, and which his shopping expedition had now made possible.

It perhaps goes without saying that his mind's eye was now as much, if not more, impaired in natural function than either of his non-metaphorical eyes. There is no need to keep the reader in a state of suspense over Buckrack's mental disorder when we are actually able, beyond what any neurologist might theorise or MRI scan display about his damaged brain, to make ourselves privy to his very thought processes. But still, language lets us down. One wishes that twenty-first century prose could do more poetic justice to his derangement – could describe it more gothically, let us say[31] – than is actually possible in an age in which terms like *paraphrenia, encephalotrigeminal angiomatosis* and *micropsia* comprise the appropriate vocabulary. Let us simply acknowledge that, with his pre-frontal cortex increasingly going to porridge, Buckrack was rapidly descending into what modern-day psychiatrists have (unwittingly wittily) called *intermittent explosive disorder*.[32]

He had, as we can appreciate, plenty of cogent reasons to be full of rage. It is no fun at all to have your braincase banjaxed and then be thrown immediately into a merciless, lonely drama of mere survival: it's madman-on-the-heath stuff, leads to a pointed sense of injustice, and makes mindless revenge appear a sober desideratum. There is a stage at which rage, arising as it may out of a certain emotional logic, becomes a besetting apoplexy, a caution-eradicating possession of

[31] One suspects that the many and purple descriptions of insanity in Poe are once more being wistfully invoked (indeed, Frederick Usher is likewise described as having a "mental disorder" before his author's habitually lush language gets the better of him).

[32] One should point out, on the other hand, that Buckrack was hardly free of vindictive, nay, murderous intent even before his brain was tenderized by McNamara's arcing meat-softener (whose parabola through the air, itself the cause of Buckrack's cerebral dysfunction, is a neatly symmetrical manifestation of a less recurrent ultraviolent syndrome in McNamara). But then, there's a lot of this about in the world of Odium, so much that it appears to be one of its organising principles: we have witnessed even Redman taking pleasure in a brutal, albeit imaginary, massacre of persons. Clockman can surely be indicted on moral grounds for potentially raising in prospective students the fear that they will not so much enjoy life at university as risk a savage death there.

the man by maniacal drives, convulsions of his normal sensibilities which convince him that unregulated destruction will set everything to rights, or at least equalise the wrongs. So thought Buckrack now.

All of which explains what he did shortly afterwards, when his newly acquired mobile phone pinged to signify that it was connected to the network. He called up a web page, entered a code, and listened to the recordings of Dethbridge talking to his CIA handler, made by the bug McNamara had earlier reinstalled in Asterisk's office. He sent these by anonymous FTP to McNamara's email address. Then, phone in hand, he unlocked the door of the basement and walked down the stairs.

"Havva photogra ya. Send to McNama," he told Asterisk in his slurring speech.

Asterisk stood up, relieved to have something to do.

Buckrack seemed to have decided that the artificial light in the basement was sufficient. "No," he sighed tersely, holding aside the phone, disapproving of Asterisk's instinctive attempt to smile. "Loo misable."

Asterisk complied by affecting a frown. The photo was taken. He was puzzled by the fact that Buckrack was wearing rubber gloves, but even more surprised, as he turned to leave, to be invited to follow him upstairs for a change of scenery for an hour. "Bu behay yassel."

He climbed the stairs gratefully after the American, who stood at the top, waiting for him. He was hoping that he might be able to engage Buckrack in some humanising conversation. But as Asterisk's shoe was on the top step, the other man unexpectedly lunged at him with the side of his body foremost, barging into him with force and sending him reeling backwards. Asterisk lost his footing and rattled down the staircase on his back, his head thumping several times on the serried steps. The fall did not knock him entirely unconscious, but immobilised and disorientated him as he lay, half on the cellar floor.

He heard the ungainly clumping of footsteps coming back down the stairs, accompanied by solid grunts of strenuous effort, saw a quick flash of thin blue rope and minatory shadows, and then his trachea was painfully constricted, there were lights flashing in his stressed vision, he was gasping for air and not finding it, and his last thoughts before he departed this earth were that he was never going to enjoy a single day of his pension and would die intestate, even though he did not have a loved one to leave anything to.

Chapter Eleven

McNamara slept deeply for about three hours and was awoken only by the alarm he had set on his phone. Picking it up, bleary-eyed, he saw a text message on the screen which he was able to read after reaching for his glasses: "Photo. Also check email." He tapped through and noted the picture of a grim-looking Asterisk, in an unidentifiable location, time-stamped at 5.51pm. He opened his email and followed the generic instructions to download the three short audio files, to which he listened with a certain mordant satisfaction at the evidence they provided of Dethbridge's complicity with his CIA interlocutor.

He got up and took a shower and was downstairs by 8.30pm. From the kitchen came the smell of lightly burned food. From Drusilla, when he found her looking bemused and happy in the lounge, came the tangy smell of alcohol. At first he thought she was still merely merry, but after a few sentences of conversation he discovered that she was quite far gone. She seemed, nonetheless, to be in a very self-satisfied mood.

"Maybe let up on the botanicals," he said, indicating the drink in her hand. "Tomorrow may be a gruelling day."

She snickered. "Izzat what you did last night when you got so plastered you blacked out?"

"Up to you," he replied. "But how did you know about that?"

She smiled sardonically. "Redman."

"You spoke to James?"

"Yeah," she affirmed, and then added, "he called me about the redundancies."

"Oh," he remarked, "yes."

There was the silence that often intervenes in the discourse between a drunk and a sober person.

"Didn't you say," Drusilla garbled, "that you had a meeting?"

"I did." He bestirred himself, put on his jacket, and made to leave. "I'll see you later."

"I'll sleep in one of the spare rooms," she said. "Probably go to bed soon. Have to get up at six. Do not disturb."

"Okay," he agreed, and left.

He took the path round the side of the house through the long private garden that led down to the rear of the Trump Building. His sleep had been hugely restorative, and a sense of command was back in place. It was night, the sun having dipped below the horizon but its light still hanging like a bright sheet in the May sky, and warm, the many carefully tended flowers that lined his walk giving off honeyed scents and a feeling of abundant pleasure which had been missing in his recent days.

The "lawyer" who appeared in his office at the appointed time, escorted by security, was exactly what he expected from the narrative genre in which he now reluctantly accepted that he was an actor. McNamara enjoyed binge-watching contemporary television spy series, especially the ones which emphasised the bureaucratic dimensions of espionage agencies more than their sensational aspects, because these reminded him so much of life in a modern university. His appetite for them was sufficiently great that he had even graduated from the more obvious ongoing English-language specimens like *The Americans* and *Homeland* to obscurer subtitled examples like *Deutschland 83* and *Fauda*. It was often a struggle to tolerate the many ludicrous plot holes and incredible twists of events that took place in the dramatically simplified reality of these imagined worlds, but they were nonetheless far more believable creations than the childishly exaggerative forerunners he had seen on the TV of his youth. He found that their wish-fulfilling shortcomings could be negotiated tolerably if they were counterbalanced by a sufficient quantity of humdrum human incompetence, error and inadequacy, as in *Le Bureau des Légendes*, whose second season he had recently finished watching. And so it was with some gratification that he noted that the woman now sitting across the desk from him – who had introduced herself as Ava Blunt – looked rather like the character Marie-Jeanne in the French drama:[33] fortyish, hair dyed because probably greying, plain, neatly but unremarkably dressed in a dark skirt and jacket, with an air of professionalism (and also, no doubt, an active microphone in her pocket and a knowing attitude when it came to civilian suckers like him). He determined to make it clear early on that he was no sucker.

[33] The trilogy seems to be getting high on its own obsession with marijuana in these two slang-infused female names.

"I won't ask you to get your phone and turn it off," he said. "I know they can listen in even when that is so."

"I beg your pardon?" she replied.

McNamara smiled weakly. "Whoever it is, wherever they are – London, Langley, both?"

Ava Blunt gave a slight inclination of the head and narrowing of the eyes that, he thought, might have been convincing in amateur theatre. McNamara said, "There is no need to keep up the pretence of being a lawyer."

"But I am a lawyer," she replied.

"Where did you study?" he asked.

She replied, "Cornell, then the LSE."

"What year did you graduate?"

"From Cornell?"

"From both."

"1997, then 2001."

"You did a Ph.D.?"

"Yes."

"Who was your supervisor?"

"Professor Arnold goddamn Schwarzenegger," she laughed, drily and humourlessly. "You'll be asking me next what my thesis was about. But you can find all that out by Googling me. I am not here to prove my *bona fides*, sir. I am here to discuss the case before us."

McNamara sighed and reached for his own phone on the desk. He pressed a button on the audio app and, on speaker, let Elfyn Dethbridge's side of the recorded conversations between him and Ava Blunt play out loud. As they did so he put a hand into a desk drawer and picked out the bug he had retrieved from Asterisk's office on his way into the building. He put it on the desk and stopped the playback. "Your property, I believe," he said, pushing the listening device an inch or two forward. "Standard CIA issue, I am informed."

Ava Blunt said nothing. She looked intently at the little grey box sitting on the desktop.

"You know I once taught the current UK Foreign Secretary?" McNamara went on. "You probably do. He phones me up occasionally. I have his number in my contacts. I wonder what he'd be forced to say or do if I revealed to him that the CIA had bugged my Registrar's office and was dealing duplicitously with my Deputy Registrar, as well as lodging confected lawsuits in the names of people who no longer exist, with ulterior motives, against a public institution, not to speak of impersonating a British policeman."

The lawyer still resisted comment.

McNamara leaned in towards the listening device. "Hello, Langley. Perhaps you could tell Ms Blunt in her earpiece what to say, as she seems lost for words? It's not quite going to script here." Then he sat back and folded his arms and stared.

Blunt put out her hand and turned the switch on the bug off, taking it and placing it in her handbag. Then she delved into her jacket pocket, took out her phone and did something on its screen. Finally, she reached into her ear and removed a small dark capsule, showed it to McNamara, and then put it also in her purse.

"Jesus," he said. "I was joking. You actually do have an earpiece and they really are listening in. Luckily, I don't care."

"You don't care?" Blunt repeated.

"Not about the lawsuit or the fact that you are CIA," he said. "But the ulterior motives, in those I may be interested. Are you going to tell me what they are, or do I have to guess? I may have ulterior motives of my own, although I assure you they are trivial in comparison to what I think yours are. Or I guess now that I have let you retrieve your property you could simply leave, and disappear, hopefully to intrude no more."

"I see no problem," she replied, "in hearing your guess."

"You want Buckrack, or the guy who goes by that name," McNamara stated flatly. "You've wanted him ever since you planted that device on our premises. I can't tell you exactly where he is, but I can give you the new mobile phone number he used to contact me in the last few hours. That should be enough to make your trail go warm. He said he'd be contacting me on a spoof number but it looks pretty much like a regular one to me. He told me he's injured and laid up and wants to buy time to make his plans. Unfortunately he has kidnapped Nigel Asterisk, my Registrar, and has been holding him hostage since earlier today. So either I let you try to deal with it or, if you don't, I call the police right after you leave here. I am guessing you don't want me doing the latter because you'd have involved them long before if you were comfortable with that, instead of pretending actually to be them instead. You presumably want to deal with Buckrack yourselves rather than let him fall into the hands of the British authorities."

Blunt considered and finally said, "When did he contact you?"

"Just before 6pm. He sent me an image of Asterisk by text."

"So," Blunt said, "why haven't you called the police already?"

"I was waiting to meet with you," McNamara answered. "If I involve the police then the whole thing goes public and this University suffers another massive reputational nosedive. You might be able to be more discreet, and probably more direct and effective."

"I see," Blunt said. "I understand. So, you wanna give me the number?"

"I'd be happy to," said McNamara. "But I need a formal letter withdrawing this spurious lawsuit, so that I don't have to report on it. I'd also like some elucidation on a couple of things. Like, why do you want him so badly? What did he do?"

"I can get a letter emailed to you almost instantly, certainly by morning." Blunt then took a breath and spoke in a way that seemed to commit herself much further. "We believe that Buckrack, as he likes you to think of him, murdered your predecessor, Sir Evan Covet, as well as an American citizen, Jane Blake. Buckrack's son had an extra-marital affair with Blake and killed himself when this fact was about to be made public. Buckrack found the son's body. He thus had strong motive to revenge himself on Jane Blake and he deliberately put himself in a position where he had ample opportunity. We couldn't prove any of this in a court of law but, yes, we can't risk someone with his detailed knowledge of our work falling into British hands. We need to secure him and get him off the scene. We've been trying to do so for months."

McNamara grunted softly in an attempt to disguise the internal impact these revelations had on him. They were of greater magnitude than he had expected.

"If we manage to do that, it solves your problem also," Blunt continued. "As for your kidnapped coll-eague, I'd agree with you that he has a better chance of survival if you let us deal with it quickly, in our way."

McNamara lifted his phone and toyed with it. "There's one other thing, also minor in comparison. Your involvement with Elfyn Dethbridge, the way you used him, how you got him to act on your behalf. Did you bribe him? I need to know."

Blunt shook her head. "We *persuaded* him."

"How?"

After the briefest of pauses Blunt answered, "I can airdrop you the video."

Buckrack did not play chess, but at his Great Game he had been no patzer: he had initiated espionage combinations which would have earned the respect of a Capablanca, if not a Botvinnik.[34] He had skewered and pinned and epauletted his opponents with practised

---

[34] The suggestion seems to be that Buckrack is a world-beating grand master spy, among the most talented ever. The posthumous José Raúl Capablanca (whom we must assume is looking down on these actions between moves in a chess tournament in the heavens) may hold a certain sympathy with him because his own life ended with a catastrophic cerebral haemorrhage; the deceased Mikhail Botvinnik, a hard-line Communist who regularly acted as if his participation in international competitions was an extension of Soviet foreign policy, is unlikely to share this admiration for the ex-CIA man, though he may have a certain feeling for what we have hitherto heard from McNamara, given that he died of pancreatic cancer. But perhaps the deprecatory view of chess to be found in Edgar Allan Poe (a man whose deranged death's cause may forever lack precise specification) is really what lies behind the *mutatis mutandis* analogy: in "The Murders in the Rue Morgue" he calls chess an "elaborate frivolity" involving mere calculation as opposed to genuine intellectual analysis. Buckrack's judgment and foresight have certainly been lacking since his very first appearance in this third volume (we can now see that his forced re-emergence was like the movement of a pawn), to the degree that a couple of lost pieces of brain tissue appear now to have sent them over the edge into their opposite, unpredictable irrationality. He is no longer playing, but being played. That said, even pawns can continue to cause damage until the very moment they are sacrificed.

precision. A novelisation of his mid-career would render him more heroic than this ending tale of its tail-end. But now that his real world itself was beginning actually to look like the chequered board, all blocky black and white, he was rapidly losing his acquired abilities in strategy, either attacking or defensive.

The sequencing of his moves was now more determined by desperate impulse than consequential thinking. Since the contents of his brainbox had been rearranged, revenge for wrongs done was henceforth at the front of his mind, or what was left of it, in his decision to return from initially unintended murder scene one to now fully intended murder scene two. To be sure, he had not lost entirely the spy's ingrained tendency to pursue the course of ruthless action which secures his aim most effectively: getting rid of McNamara as well as Asterisk would eliminate the two sources of first-hand information about him, as they were the only two people to whom he had recently made himself known. Once that was accomplished, it would afford him greater latitude to fade away undetected, to be the wandering ghost he had played surpassingly well until his current remedial revisitation to Odium had appeared, alas mistakenly, to have become necessary. Nonetheless, the blood that pumped his energies in this direction was not as cold as it should have been. His neurovascular coupling was too impaired for this any longer to be possible.

The journey back in Asterisk's car was ordeal enough in the fading evening light. In the dark of actual night it would have been entirely unmanageable. For the most part it was like playing a driving video game on a widescreen black-and-white TV monitor that was itself on the fritz, its screen flickering and jumping and its sound all muffled bass. Other vehicles hurtled past or towards him, or welled up into his vision as he approached them from the rear, like tall grey polygonal boxes (if they were vans or lorries) or streaking, low-lying slits of dim light (if they were cars). It was at times like running as a jackal at dusk in the middle of one vast pack, with a different pack coming the other way, in both of which giant and very speedy buffalo had got mixed up. Luckily most of it was motorway and he was able to settle in the slow lane and devote all his fraught concentration to obeying its gentle curves and cambers without the need to negotiate turns, traffic lights or urban multi-directionality. Even so, a journey that would usually last two hours took him almost three and a half, including two unscheduled breaks forced upon him by heart palpitations that arose from near accidents. By the time he parked on the road to the north of McNamara's campus home there was only a fading glow across the sky.

His plan had been to search for a ground-floor window left open against the early summer heat, or at least unlocked. He found none, but on the last explored wall of the house he saw, at ankle level, the cellar skylight from which he had escaped in the early hours of that morning. The broken glass had been cleaned out from the edges of the frame but the pane had not yet been replaced. The gap had simply been temporarily boarded up. On a chance that the cellar door inside had been left unlocked, he tried the board with his foot. It certainly seemed to give with moderate pressure. Getting onto the floor on his side, he jackknifed his legs and plunged the soles of both feet against the flimsy planking and satisfyingly felt it collapse. It did not spring away entirely and fall back into the subterranean room, but the tacks securing its top had burst loose along the edge and the wood had bowed inwards in a way that required him only to push at it firmly on both sides and lever it away. With the light board still in his hand he leaned in and was able to place it quietly inside. Then, with some grunts and stiff-limbed awkwardness, he got his body in after it.

There was now a bare modicum of late evening light coming in from his entrance, but as far as Buckrack was concerned, with his scrambled vision, it was almost total blackout in the cellar. The two things he could just make out were the faint luminosity from the gutted window whence he had come and, more hearteningly, a faint sliver of domestic light glimmering under the door at the top of the staircase where he wanted to go. These orientated him and allowed him to fumble and feel his way towards the bottom of the steps, which he then ascended laboriously on all fours, like a dog. He uprighted himself at the top and let the palm of his hand drift about the surface of the wall around the door, but could find no light switch. He then groped around the door itself at waist height and eventually identified its rounded handle. He turned it anti-clockwise, experimentally, and felt its sprung-action mechanism twist without hindrance. This suggested that it had not been re-locked on the other side. With the handle turned fully to the left, he applied some gentle inward force. But the door did not budge. He released the handle carefully and pressed an ear against the surface of the door. He could hear nothing from the house beyond. To be surer, because his hearing had been increasingly defective, he turned his face and pressed the other ear to it, with the same reassuring non-result. He took hold of the door handle and turned it once more and pulled again. He felt the faintest of shudders in its length. It seemed that the door had fallen a little on its hinges and that its bottom edge was in contact with the floor at the handle end. It was a sticky door, not a locked one. Buckrack took a deep breath, reached into his jacket pocket and fetched out the length of rope he had concealed there. Then he gave the door the kind of firm, positive tug he felt it would require to open it.

The unexpected events which occurred immediately thereafter took all of thirty seconds but had the slow-motion, lumbering qualities of a frantic dream. The door overcame the resistant force of the floor and opened with a noisy scrape, then jammed again when only six inches ajar. Buckrack momentarily saw in the hallway a black silhouette in motion, framed against bright white light from the kitchen beyond. He could not make out who it was, but the darkened human form could clearly see him, for he felt the light fully on his face. The other person froze and let fall to the floor a tumbler: there was the short, soft, gurgling sound of decanting liquid. The door was not yet open wide enough for Buckrack to pass through, so instinctively he began to struggle with it. Just as he did so the body in the interior lobby launched itself towards him with the seeming intention of crashing against the door and sending him flying backwards down the cellar staircase. At the last moment he managed to wrench the barricade fully open, but not soon enough to avoid the full bodily collision that ensued. For a split second in a freeze-frame world the open-armed Buckrack seemed to receive human contact in what looked like a pass-ionate embrace. In the very next an anatomical chaos of interpersonally concatenated limbs and clanging heads and convulsing lungs and cracking ribs and kicking legs was cascading down the wooden companionway into the penumbrous bowels of the basement.

Miraculously, Buckrack found that he landed on top, and from the depths of his physical being found the wherewithal to overcome the concussions of the descent and reach down towards the barely visible face he knew was beneath him. He then howled in pain as he felt teeth clamp shut on two of his fingers, which he had to unplug with rubber-glove-finger-shredding agony from the mouth which had taken them prisoner. He felt blood rising to his face and adrenalin surging at his heart, giving him a new rush of strength with which he looped the length of cord in his hand around his antagonist's collar, flipped one end under the other to form a half knot and, ignoring the trauma inflicted on his bitten fingers, pulled both ends savagely away from each other as tightly as he could.

Drusilla Frost, her system awash with alcoholic spirits, did not experience much in the way of discernible pain. It was all over too quickly for that. Her head seemed to swell with liquid pressure, which is the predictable consequence of garroted carotids. As her windpipe collapsed with a faint cracking wheeze, she was preoccupied with two final reflections that vied for her attention. The first occasioned outraged surprise: she was, ridiculously, going to die before her elderly, senile, terminally ill mother. The second plunged her, in the single instant she countenanced it, into an infinite-seeming despair whose actual hold upon her living soul proved at least mercifully brief: never again would she feel the thunderous thwack of James Redman's dyadic ivory snooker balls against the wide-open pocket of her perinaeum. No one's life deserved to end like this, in a mere one-one draw between *la petite mort* and *la grande mort*, she might have vowed to argue with God or the Devil, had she not been regrettably ignorant of those expressive French idioms.[35]

Drusilla could have learned some things from Ava Blunt. A woman who routinely slings a .38 calibre pistol in a holster against her left breast can be expected to have meditated on the relation between sex and death. At the very least she knew that she wanted, Jim Morrison-like, to have her kicks before the whole shithouse went up in flames. And so her CIA-governed life was actually very like that delineated in similar characters in some TV series: in order to balance out the discipline and patience required by serious professional espionage, her personal life was a catastrophic

[35] I do not belong (it should be clear by now) to that astringent, ascetic, slavish school of critics which demands that we accept a text as it is. I rather prefer to point out where an author could have done better. At first reading I immediately considered how this callously erudite speculation might have been more cynically multi-layered by some additional authorial and well cadenced observation that Drusilla passed into death as mono-linguistically as she had experienced life only mono-orgasmically, until I remembered that we are told (in the second volume) that she is at least transactionally competent in Chinese. Still, if one is going to lather on the comedy in the midst of morbidity, which is the unruly tendency this novel relentlessly pursues, one might have added in a subordinate clause, "despite the French lesson given to her by Redman that afternoon". This would fittingly have transformed a mono-witticism, as it were, into a multi-witticism. But one senses that our author, unlike the sensuous, epicurean, Redmanish lover, is somewhat rushing to get to the end of the matter. The textual multiplicity we are offered is mere narratological repetition: not a mono-murder in a cellar, but multi-murders in cellars.

disorder of short-term gratification and thoughtless excess, particularly in the sexual sphere. She was discovering that the forties was a good age, or at least good for her, because she was now senior enough to be mentoring relatively new entrants to the profession, most of whom were male and did not seem to know quite how to repel her usually very direct sexual harassment of them, or gave in to it for invidious reasons, or accepted it because for some the mere availability of sex will do even if genuine attraction is absent, or because they were just horny.

Which of these applied to Bradley Drumm, the twenty-nine-year old ex-Harvard frat boy on whose crotch she sometimes stroked the palm of her right hand as he drove them to Buckinghamshire, she neither knew nor cared. But she knew that Brad just adored the idea of a woman being so coquettish as to fool around with his cock and balls while he was driving a car (or undo her shirt buttons and flash a naked tit in his direction) and couldn't wait to boast to his friends. He pretended to blush, but she was sure he loved her iterating aloud what she was going to do with him, or rather to his genitals, when they got back to London after tonight's operation. And who among us, on the way to commit an extra-judicial murder, could say that they would not welcome such blatant, forthright distractions from everyday conduct? Given how events panned out in the rest of the night, no one would reasonably begrudge Blunt or Drumm such death-deferring lascivious foreplay.

The fact that the phone number McNamara had provided had led, when Blunt ran it through Langley, to a live connection at the actual address where the dead bodies of Sir Evan Covet and Jane Blake had been discovered six months before, was entirely convincing to her and her handlers back at HQ. Consent for her to proceed there immediately with Drumm and put an end to this vexing matter was given without demur, despite the lateness of the hour or indeed perhaps because of it: the target might arise and disappear by daybreak. It was perhaps the fact, the relief, the achievement of having at last actually fixed Buckrack's location in real time, after so many months of trying, that led the entire team handling the case to suppress their doubts about the ease with which they had been allowed to do so. Unaccountably, there was no conversation with Blunt as to why Buckrack, one of their own, had been so lax with his phone number or left the mobile switched on and so readily discoverable that Langley was able to hack its mic and listen in as Blunt and Drumm approached the house at around quarter-past midnight, she taking the front, he the rear, each giving whispered running commentary to HQ using bluetooth headsets connected to their own phones.

The listeners back at Langley had only the multiple audio to go on. But it was in the end lack of audio, an uninterrupted rustic nocturnal silence from every device, that finally told them that something must have gone terribly wrong. When they later replayed the recordings they thought they detected a similar pattern of sounds just after the two agents had tried to enter the property: front and rear doors were opened within seconds of each other, there was at both then a gentle noise like a creak, then a whoosh as of something travelling fast through air, which ended abruptly with a muffled thud which had also a bit of a flesh-and-blood squelch to it.

Thereafter there was absolutely nothing. Neither

agent replied to the increasingly fretful entreaties that crossed the Atlantic and were transmitted, seemingly unheard, into their ears.

Langley roused someone in London (the very agent who had impersonated Detective Superintendent Nesbit in Asterisk's office two days before), got him into a car speeding towards Buckinghamshire to find out what disaster had befallen. But it was too late. HQ cut the connection with the agents' phones and remote wiped them as soon as they detected sounds of activity near them, about half an hour later, leaving live only the hacked mic on the phone Buckrack had left switched on inside the house. It told them little more than their man up from the capital was able to confirm from what he could see upon his arrival: the local police in the form of Detective Superintendent Nesbit and his assistants were already present on the scene.

Chapter Twelve

After the departure from his office of Ava Blunt,
McNamara found himself slowly filling with a certain
kind of joy. It was, to be sure, mainly the negative
contentment of absent pains rather than the positive
pleasure of present achievements, but that is what most
men of his age are content to aspire to. He had just
acquired information that would allow him to punish
Elfyn Dethbridge, that obnoxious mosquito who had
buzzed infuriatingly around his life beyond endurance;
he had helped set in train events which might save
Nigel Asterisk's life, a virtuous act which he did not
consider undermined by the fact that he felt no
particular responsibility for it and did not personally
care one way or the other if it were to be snuffed out in
the crossfire of an imagined shooting match (such an
outcome would spare McNamara a degree of testy
administrative bother, but on balance he hoped against
Asterisk's death on account of the woeful press coverage that would inevitably follow it). He presumed
there was a strong chance that the CIA might now rid
the world of its and his Buckrack problem without noise
or fuss, and he also considered himself not to have lost
face in his direct dealings with them; above all, he could

just about envisage the prospect that the University of Odium and his stewardship of it might not be mentioned in any further adverse public discussion, that the chain of troubles unleashed by the unruly American first invited onto campus by Sir Evan Covet may well now run out to an unremarkable end. He did not dwell on the objective truth that he was the Vice Chancellor of the University of Odium largely as an accident borne of Buckrack's many pestilential deeds; he preferred to consider how his position would be quietly consolidated if no more such deeds were possible.

He was the opposite of tired, close to chipper; he would have to wait until the next morning to exult in firing Dethbridge; Drusilla, drunk, had said she would be sleeping in a guest room; yet the warm early summer evening had a slightly magical feel to it which he wanted to prolong in company, and it was not very late. So he called Redman and proposed a nightcap and a catch-up. The younger man tried to cry off the proposed meeting, said he was exhausted. But McNamara was insistent and used to applying the moral pressure that often worked on subordinates, saying he needed some advice and that it couldn't wait, that he was prepared to come over to his place, and hinting that a confidential preview of the next instalment of the Odium soap opera (particularly as it affected the Registrar's department) was also on offer. Redman acceded. McNamara called the Security Office and asked them to order him a taxi.

But Redman was no fun. He did not even take a drink and seemed ill-at-ease. Perhaps he was weary after all, but it seemed to McNamara more that his mind was preoccupied with something else, so much so that even the dangled mention of the likely upcoming dismissals of Asterisk and Dethbridge did not appear to pique his interest. Finding him a wet blanket, McNamara returned home after a couple of hours, idly watched TV for a while to catch up with the news, took a sleeping pill and went to bed.

He was not actually woken by the unusual early morning knocking at the door: he had his dawn porter, Chivers, to see to such unpredictable occurrences.[36] Evidently this was not someone Chivers could turn away, however, for it was the batman's subsequent assertive banging on his bedroom door that tugged McNamara out of his Zopiclone-induced mini-coma. The groggy laird of the manor did not quite catch the explanation which he thought was uttered by Chivers from the upstairs hallway before retreating once his unwelcome alarum call had been acknowledged. McNamara glanced blearily at his phone and saw that it was only some minutes after seven o'clock. Given the earliness of the hour he decided that a dressing gown over his pyjamas would be sufficient.

Downstairs, in the large dining room, he encountered a familiar face floating above the surface of the table. It smiled at him.

"Well, hello," McNamara said, barely concealing his puzzlement.

"Remember me?" came the reply. The man stood up to shake hands.

"Yes. Yes, of course. Mr Nesbit, right? We spoke on the phone yesterday."

---

[36] And so the Covet-Frost-McNamara circle is closed by their explicit Shakespearian inter-association: they all come, so to speak, to feel their titles hang loose about them, like a giant's robe upon a dwarfish thief.

"Detective Superintendent Nesbit, Buckinghamshire CID, yes. I am sorry to trouble you at home so early."

McNamara mumbled an offer of coffee, but Nesbit indicated that Chivers was already taking care of that.

"Is it something to do with the Evan Covet case?" McNamara thought aloud, his mind beginning to race.

Nesbit grimaced. "If only it were," he lamented. "No, no, it's rather more recent than that, though perhaps, we might find out, related."

McNamara noticed with some discomfort that Nesbit was regarding him in a studious manner. He ran a hand through his hair and sat down. "How can I help?" he asked.

"Your Registrar," Nesbit began. "Nigel Asterisk."

McNamara was waiting for a question but this toneless utterance was all Nesbit vouchsafed for the moment. Eventually he mustered what he hoped sounded like a reply ignorant of all data that could possibly have brought Nesbit here to talk to him in connection with Nigel Asterisk. "Yes, what about him?"

Laconically Nesbit answered, "He's dead."

McNamara did not need to perform his reaction. He felt the blood drain naturally from his face. Fortunately Chivers punctured the silence by bringing in the coffee, which allowed the hiatus to pass in an awkward domestic ceremony of pouring and clinking.

McNamara found himself staring down into his coffee cup with a hand on his forehead. "Good God. But I saw him only yesterday," he said slowly, then looked up. "Oh what, are you asking me to identify another body, like the last time?"

"No, no, that won't be necessary, not now at any rate," Nesbit reassured him. "We're fairly certain of the ID, he had plenty on his person, enough to leave it in little doubt. I will fill you in on the details in a moment, if you can be patient with me. You say you last saw him yesterday. May I ask when yesterday?"

"Late morning. I sent him home."

"Oh, was he ill?"

"Er, no, that's not quite it. How can I explain? We're in the midst of a major restructuring and Nigel's, er, well, his recent performance of his duties has been problematic. He was suspended pending disciplinary investigation."

"I see," said Nesbit, making a note in his notepad. "So, what, that would be around 11am, or after?"

"Maybe nearer noon."

"So that was quite some time before you called and left me a message?"

"Yes, but my calling you turned out to be an error."

"You thought I had spoken with Dr Asterisk and had made a request of him to see your purchasing records."

"Yes, well, no, what I mean is ... Nigel has – *had* – been in a very stressed condition of late, I believe, and we were uncovering many instances in which his judgment had become extremely confused. This turned out to be yet another one. I am not at all sure how he got the idea in his head that you had made any such request. I was simply acting on the facts as they had been relayed to me. They turned out not to be true."

"I see. And did you speak to him later in the day?"

McNamara gave the impression of considering this carefully. "I did, yes. He texted me and asked me to call him. Do you mind if I check my phone?"

"Go ahead. I think you'll find that he texted you shortly after you and I spoke. You then called him back and he did not answer. Then he called you back and you spoke for about ten minutes."

McNamara's eyes widened. "You've already done a check on my phone logs?" He looked at his call list. The policeman was accurate in his knowledge.

Nesbit shrugged apologetically. "It's part of the routine these days, sir. And it's why I'm here now. We find a dead man and yours is the last number he called. We're bound to check it out. But we only know that calls were made and the time they were made and how long they lasted. We don't know the content of those calls. Do you mind telling me what you discussed? And did he say where he was?"

McNamara exhaled, then stopped and looked at Nesbit quizzically. "Hang on, where did you find him? Why on earth was he in Buckinghamshire?"

"I'll come to that in a moment. It's one of the things we need to try to understand. Can you tell me what passed between you in your last conversation?"

"Nothing of any moment. He was upset about being suspended, wanted reassurance about the disciplinary procedure, or to see if he could avoid it, felt the need to apologise, said he would try and make amends. But mostly he just seemed in a state of understandable nervous anxiety."

"And did you have any contact from him after that?"

"I did. It was rather strange." McNamara checked on his phone, as there was no getting around the data it contained. "It was sent to me shortly before 6pm and was just a texted photo of him, but it came from an unrecognised number."

Nesbit dug out a phone and fiddled with it then showed the screen to McNamara. An undead Asterisk looked sombrely back at him.

"Was this the photo?" Nesbit asked.

"Yes," said McNamara.

"To be honest, if you say that's him, we've pretty much positively confirmed the ID. Can I ask, how did you react when you received this photo?"

"Well, I didn't see it 'til around eight-thirty, when I woke up. I had taken an early evening sleep."

"And?"

McNamara shrugged. "I didn't know what to make of it. As I say, he'd been behaving unpredictably."

"You didn't call the number back to ask?"

"No," McNamara said. "By that time at night I tend to leave things until the following morning, to be honest, and I suppose I just thought it was, well, a bit weird, but then, as I say, he's been a bit weird of late."

"When you say *weird*," Nesbit probed, "what kind of conduct do you mean?"

"Several things," McNamara said. "Poor judgments, stressed-out behaviour, paranoia. But, you know, these are not altogether unusual in a senior manager in a university, periodically, anyway."

"I see," said Nesbit. "And can you think of any recent reason why he may have been this way?"

"Well, not particularly, but between you and me, we are at the start of a major redundancy process, so tensions are, er, higher than usual. And that has been brought about partly as a result of the reputational hit we took from the bad press about the deaths you investigated at the end of last year. Nigel had to deal with the aftermath of all that. I haven't talked to him about it in detail – it's a subject we all try to avoid, to be honest – but I imagine it took its toll."

Nesbit nodded. He seemed to be accepting the repetitive clichéd generalities he was receiving amiably enough. "Do you know if he was taking Valium?" he threw in.

McNamara shook his head. "I'll admit that Nigel and I were not the closest of colleagues."

"Still," Nesbit sighed, "it fits what you say. We found some on him."

There was a lull.

"You were going to give me some more details?" McNamara reminded him. "It would be helpful to know what happened. I may have to prepare some kind of statement. I mean, was it an accident?"

"Oh, well, this is the thing, no. He was violently killed. Strangled."

McNamara went doubly ashen.

"I know it's a shock," said Nesbit, "but there's a more shocking thing. Do you recognise the place in the photo at all?"

"No," said McNamara truthfully.

"It's Sir Evan Covet's house. The same one where he and Jane Blake were found dead."

McNamara's head sank slowly into his hands, half in bewilderment, half in meditation. Nesbit concluded that the Vice Chancellor was momentarily speechless, and went on. "Now, quite what that means I currently have no idea. It could very possibly be some outlandish copy-cat thing, someone knows the house where two deaths took place is empty, decides for some bizarre reason to create another death there, but then, how did they gain entry without breaking in, and why would Dr Asterisk be there? And it's too much to believe it's a mere coincidence that Dr Asterisk works at your University too. Is it possible he had a key?"

McNamara looked back at the detective. "I'm sorry, I just don't know."

"I am waiting," Nesbit went on, "for a pathology report later this morning, but first indications are that he was killed maybe six, seven hours before his body was found. That's about the same time that someone sent you a photo of him. You have no idea who that could have been?"

McNamara looked blank. "When I saw the photo I simply assumed he had taken it himself," he lied.

"The phone it was taken with is registered in his name, and was bought with his debit card just a few hours before in Aylesbury. It was found in the clothes he was wearing, switched on." Nesbit seemed to be pursuing a line of thought aloud. "Now, my working assumption has to be that someone else was applying duress to him, not least because obviously another person murdered him, but that the phone itself had been wiped clean of fingerprints and presumably placed there deliberately. No calls were made on it, just the one text sent to you, as if the phone had been bought just to make that single communication. That suggests that whoever sent the photo had thrown away or destroyed Dr Asterisk's own phone, probably to prevent its location being traceable. They knew they would not be remaining at the house after they made the call, so they left the phone there. You saw him here around noon. You call me around two-twenty to talk about something he had mentioned about me. I call you back around two-thirty and we discover it seems to be a misunderstanding. He texts you on his own phone at approximately two-forty. He seems to be on the move by then. The call is from near the Odium ring-road. You call him back immediately but he does not pick up. About seven minutes later he returns the call in some agitation about his employment circumstances. We can place that call as having been made from a motorway service station on the southbound side of the M1.

203

Almost three hours later you are sent, out of the blue, a photo of him from an unknown number, taken in a rural cottage in Buckinghamshire, the very one in which his previous boss and your predecessor in your post died. Dr Asterisk may already have been killed by the time it was sent. This is a very odd sequence of events that calls out for explanation."

He left this suggestion hanging ponderously between them, but McNamara said nothing in response.

"Would you be prepared," Nesbit tried another tack, "to show me the text he sent you at 2.39?"

"Yes, of course." McNamara located the message and passed his phone to Nesbit, who read it aloud.

"'I have news about Buckrack.' What does that mean? Who is Buckrack?"

McNamara's mind had been racing to get up to lying-mode speed since uttering his first explicit untruth a few moments before. "He's one of our research professors. His name had come up in the redundancy nomination process but I had told Nigel I was sure this was a mistake as he was on a fixed-term contract that ends this year and so was irrelevant. He had forgotten to tell me that he had checked on it and so was simply tying up that loose end. In other words, it was simply routine business. In fact, that's the only reason I called him back, for that information."

"Hmm." Nesbit was not entirely convinced. "You think he'd just say, 'You were right about Buckrack.' This message seems to be an express invitation to call him back."

"I agree," McNamara nodded. "But, as I discovered, he did want to talk about other things, and looked at in that light, maybe that's why he phrased it that way: so that I would reply to his text." He was becoming a little flustered. "You know, Detective Superintendent, this is a lot to take in, and it's very disturbing. It's hard for me to give the most thoughtful answers to your questions when this news is just hitting me like this."

"I understand," Nesbit nodded, a little benignly, "and I do apologise. Unfortunately, in these matters it's usually imperative that we talk to people who may be able to assist us quickly, before, in fact, they get too reflective. Their instant reactions are rather important. We can always clarify them with further talks later. But I'm afraid I cannot make this any easier, because there's more. Dr Asterisk was not the only person murdered at the scene."

"Good God almighty," McNamara reacted. "When will it end?"

"When will it end?" Nesbit repeated.

"I'm a university Vice Chancellor," McNamara explained. "But I feel that I've fallen into an episode of *Inspector Morse*."

"I see what you mean," Nesbit smiled wryly, "except it's not exactly Oxford. I tend to hear more comparisons made with DCI Barnaby, myself."

"DCI Barnaby?"

"Yes, sir. *Midsomer Murders*. Set in Bucks, you see."

McNamara shook his head and blinked to indicate total ignorance of whatever was being alluded to in these references.

Nesbit pushed his phone across the table. "Brace yourself. I would not show you what follows unless I had to."

McNamara drew the phone gingerly towards him, reluctant to touch it, and put it in his field of view. He saw a photo in three-quarters profile of a woman he thought might be Ava Blunt, although he could hardly see the face because it was multiply impaled on four long-bladed kitchen knives, two in the eyes, two in the jaws. Further down, there were another two in the neck.

"What the hell is this?" McNamara demanded with genuine revulsion.

Nesbit winced in sympathy. "Last night a local villager was taking his dog for a very late stroll. When he passed the house and saw this woman standing in the front doorway in the moonlight he did not think too much of it. It was when he walked back the same way and she was still there in exactly the same posture ten minutes later that he started to sense something amiss. That's how we got called to the scene. To put it bluntly, the house was booby-trapped. When the door was opened a simple rope attached to a heavy board pulled back against the ceiling was released: a homemade hooks and wires and nails arrangement. These knives were cemented and also taped solidly into the board. It swung towards the door at head height and must pretty much instantly have killed whoever opened it. And not a single fingerprint to be discovered on the contraption. Do you have any idea who this woman is? The body was still warm when we found her, so we know that she died quite some time after Dr Asterisk."

"I can't even make out her features," McNamara answered. "There's too much blood. You haven't been able to identify her?"

Nesbit shook his head. "No personal ID on her at all. And, most oddly, her phone was entirely clean, not a single piece of data on it, which was true also of the young man who suffered the same fate at the back door. Our villager didn't know about him. We came across that extra corpse ourselves. By the time we reached your colleague in the basement we were prepared for almost anything. If you scroll a few images forward you will see the unfortunate young man."

"Do I have to? This is disgusting."

"I would be grateful if you would, on the off-chance that you can help us at all."

Bradley Drumm being somewhat taller than Ava Blunt, his eyes were at least undefiled in his deathly mugshot. They were open and seemed brimful of frozen startlement. The two top knives had stabbed him lower in the face. The two middle ones were in his throat. The lowest pair had lodged in his upper chest.

This time McNamara did not have to prevaricate. "I don't know who this guy is." He was relieved at being able to look away. "But this front-door-back-door thing, isn't that the kind of way police would enter a house?"

"Or criminals after a person," Nesbit said, reaching a hand forward to take the phone. "But, you see, whoever left these traps was obviously fearful that someone would come or at least expected them. You would think a person in that situation, or *people* if we are not to rule out the possibility that there may have been more than one, who had, I mean, gone to the lengths of purchasing a brand new phone and ensuring there were no fingerprints to evade detection, you would expect them, as I say, to be careful enough not to leave the phone so easily locatable, which is precisely what whoever bought it did. They even messaged you, which meant that someone knew the number. But you were the only person contacted on it. Only you had the number. No one else was in possession of it."

"But I didn't even speak to them," McNamara protested. "They just sent me a photo of Nigel. I had no idea why, then or now. Maybe they just did it to muddy the waters, cause confusion. They could have got my number from Nigel. Or maybe the people who sent the photo just aren't the same people who did these terrible things."

"Yes," Nesbit said, seemingly parried away by these speculations. "You are quite right there. I have of course considered that last possibility but unfortunately it is not one I can yet pursue. You can only work with the data you've got."

"I'm sorry I can't help," McNamara said. "But if you know where the phone was bought, maybe they can."

"Oh, yes, I have to get back to Aylesbury after the store opens and make those enquiries," Nesbit said, looking at his watch and getting to his feet. "There's usually CCTV footage. And we'll no doubt find out who these two sad souls are from their car registration. As for any announcement, I have to ask you to wait until we have contacted Dr Asterisk's family."

"He didn't have a family," McNamara said. "He wasn't married."

"Brothers, sisters, parents?"

"I'm fairly sure there's nobody."

"Oh dear," sighed Nesbit. "Though, looking on the bright side, that spares a lot of grief. I will check up on it and let you know when you can say something formal."

"Thank you."

"I'd be grateful if you remain contactable, you know, leave your phone on, that sort of thing, in case we have any further questions."

"Yes, of course."

Detective Superintendent Nesbit let the front door be closed behind him and stood there quietly for a moment or two. He had double-digit years in homicide cases and was too experienced to allow their usually gruesome features to disturb his *modus operandi*, which had evolved into a rough combination of logical enquiry based on a merciless suspicion of everyone, informed by the intuitive glory of instinctual hunches, all strongly tempered by what was possible within operational limits and budgets and his own variable sense of dedication. Like many professionals, Nesbit did not consider himself more than satisfactory at his job, nor did he aim to be anything higher.[37] He was not entirely content with the way in which McNamara had conducted himself in the interview. It was not that he could catch him out in any obvious lie or consciously thought that he had put on an act. It was, more surprisingly, that he had seemed too cold-blooded, not quite disgusted enough and far from sufficiently emotional at the horrific revelations. He had accepted them too readily, had not appeared amply stupefied and incredulous. The words he had said in their talk were fitting enough; but his deportment and his tone while he said them had seemed all wrong. He was not adequately shocked. People told of the murder of someone they know do not as a rule display the wits required to hypothesize about the sensational event's details: they tend more towards speechless, numbed disbelief. They are seldom as coherent as McNamara had been. He should have been stultified, but was little more than dejected.

---

[37] You don't say! After all, he readily wrote off the twin murders of Covet and Blake as a double suicide and failed ultimately to chase up Buckrack's siphoning of relevant money to an offshore account! He somewhat flatters himself, the reader must surely conclude, by daring even to cite comparisons with faultlessly successful TV-land sleuths.

Nesbit began to walk across the crunching gravel towards the squad car that had brought him here. He had left the uniformed driver on the nearby road in order not to draw attention or concern. He turned around and walked backwards, looking at the grand house largely to appreciate how the other half lived. In doing so his eye was drawn to the smashed window at foot level along the side wall. He stopped and then, his enquiry still being at the stage at which everyone and everything was to be suspected, walked over to it. By the bright morning light he saw the kicked-in board on an interior surface beneath the opening. He got onto his knees, and then gently lay horizontally on his stomach. He fished in his jacket pocket, brought out his phone and turned on its light. His head disappeared inside the frame of the broken window. Then it was gently withdrawn and he got slowly to his feet, brushing down the front of his jacket and trousers, and strode away from the house.

When he got to the roadway he did not enter the car but leaned in at the lowered passenger window and spoke to the driver.

"Get someone from Odium city homicide up here, would you?" he said. "I'm going to have to go back to get this fellow to come into the local station, but when I bring him to the car say nothing. Just keep him here until the locals arrive."

He returned to the house and knocked again with the doorclapper. This time it was McNamara who opened up, still in his dressing gown.

"I'm sorry, sir," Nesbit said. "I have just learned of some developments. I am going to have to ask you to come with us to the station here."

McNamara examined him through narrowed eyes.

210

"Are you arresting me, Detective Superintendent?"

"I hardly think that is necessary, sir," answered Nesbit. "I was rather hoping you would come of your own free will."

McNamara sighed with seeming exasperation. "May I get dressed?"

"Of course."

"Please come in and wait for me."

"Thank you." Nesbit stepped into the hallway while McNamara headed for the stairs. When he was turning on the landing, Nesbit said, "Do you live alone, sir?"

McNamara halted. "No. I live here with my partner."

"Is, er, she at home?"

"No, she's at work. She had an early start this morning."

"I see. Please don't let me keep you."

McNamara disappeared into the upper floor. Nesbit examined the closed door that must have led to the cellar and tried the handle, but it was locked and there was no key in it. He heard Chivers clunking away in the kitchen nearby.

And then there was a loud, horrified masculine yell from the top floor and a shuddering concussion on the roof above Nesbit's head which was surely, he intuited an instant later, caused by the heavy fall of an overweight human.

Chapter Thirteen

Half an hour or so later, after McNamara's prone body had been removed and whisked away in an ambulance, Nesbit stood roughly where he had found McNamara's upended feet, near one of the legs of the four-poster bed, so that he could study what the Vice Chancellor had seen when he had slid open the door of his mirrored walk-in wardrobe.

He was interrupted by the return from downstairs of his Odium equivalent, a detective named Slim, who seemed to see himself as anything but equivalent. It was Nesbit's Received Pronunciation (and the fact that he probably knew what Received Pronunciation was, which Slim did not) as well as his precedence on the scene that had thrown Slim immediately into the subordinate role in a Padawan-Master relationship he considered reassuring and untaxing on the brain: it seemed to establish order in outlandish circumstances which a midlandish brogue was ill-suited to bring under control. Slim had thus taken to speaking in nothing but questions he hoped would be answered, although he disguised his deficiency of initative by using the first person plural rather than the second person singular (which he was able to do despite his total ignorance, which Nesbit probably did not share, of the classification of grammatical persons).

"So we're sure that's the wife downstairs?" Slim said.

"Not the wife," Nesbit replied. He was not an enemy of the phatic but he disliked the redundant use of "so" at the beginning of sentences. "I don't believe they were married. He called her his partner."

"So do we have a name?"

"Drusilla Frost. Chivers told me." At Slim's look of puzzlement, Nesbit explained further. "The butler."

"Ah," Slim nodded, taking a note. "So are we taking him in for questioning?"

"Up to you," Nesbit shrugged. "It's your jurisdiction. But you don't seriously think *the butler did it*?"

Slim did not get the joke. He was not at all well versed in even the common-knowledge tropes of detective fiction. "But we don't suspect it was the husband, er, I mean, partner, is that right?"

"Professor McNamara? Well, it's true that there's something a bit fishy about his story which, if I were you, I'd probe," Nesbit said. "But you don't strangle someone in your own basement and leave them in full view and just go off to bed when you know a servant will be round first thing in the morning, do you? And though there may be the odd exception somewhere in history, affluent buggers like heads of universities don't appear to stoop to murder with repetitive regularity. Also, our man in the wardrobe here, he has an appropriate length of rope in his pocket which will probably have his and her DNA all over it, and I'm pretty sure we'll find that his DNA is all over her too, not to mention that he might have used that same rope on another victim just yesterday. And then there's the pieces of rubber in her mouth, which are obviously from the damaged glove he's still wearing. It looks to me like he broke in, killed the woman, and then concealed himself in here to await our Vice Chancellor. But he gently faded away before his intentions could be realised. Perhaps he was peckish and found something barely edible in the wardrobe that was actually rat poison. As usual, the post-mortem and forensics will probably tell us everything. Can't do much more with him until they arrive. But I'd certainly put money on him being your murderer, and probably mine as well. Which makes it a nice closed case for both of us, the perp having joined the choir invisible."[38]

[38] The literary reader may consider the last comment a deliberate piece of learned condescension on Nesbit's part (Slim is most unlikely to recognise an allusion to a poem by George Eliot) were it not for the fact that Nesbit, despite his private linguistic pedantry, is not himself much of a reader but just sounds to the plebeian Slim like he might be one: actually, Nesbit thinks "joined the choir invisible" was first coined in the *Monty Python* "dead parrot" sketch. He is a kind of parrot himself, for he often repeats the unexamined popular opinion that *Monty Python* is the pinnacle of modern humour. This is why he possesses the complete DVD box set, which he repeatedly watches whenever he wishes to contemplate the heights to which he thinks comedic genius can, at its utmost, reach. His knowledge of the literary classics, likewise, is based entirely on watching film and TV adaptations. As if all of this were not worrying enough, he here confirms his penchant for "solving" – rather, *dis*solving – murders by attributing them to already dead people (Covet, Buckrack) and thus avoiding all the bureaucratic and footleather-destroying effort usually incurred in bringing them to trial. These people have often themselves been murdered, yet their murders he neglects even to posit, never mind pursue. His completion rate on high profile homicide cases consequently made him a living legend in the Buckinghamshire force. He is renowned for having proven more dead people to have been murderers than he has apprehended living ones.

"And do we know who he is?"

Nesbit suppressed a sigh. Superfluous "ands" at the beginning of sentences he also found an irritant. "Not yet," he said. "Clean as a whistle in the ID department. But that's part of the pattern in this particular wallpaper, isn't it?"

Slim looked around the room. He could not see any wallpaper. The walls were entirely painted in magnolia. But he said nothing.

"The interesting question," Nesbit went on, "is how he got into the state he's in. He's not a pretty sight, is he? He's been through the wringer. What was his motive? Still, can't complain. This is a day for the memoirs. Five stiffs in two separate locations within an eight-hour period. My previous record was three in two days. And the visuals, well, what can one say? Stunning."

Both spent a solemn moment admiring the grotesque spectacle of the dead man in the wardrobe. He was sitting against the dim back wall with his legs outstretched in stained trousers. At some point, most likely when his body had given up the ghost, his upper half had slumped forward a little and his jaw had thus dropped open, giving him a doltish, drooling, gap-toothed look. The black-rimmed eyeballs, still open, were no longer vitreous but clouding over, like two egg whites just at the moment heat starts to affect them. The skull was badly dented on the top and the side, the hair matted and tangled with caked blood, the skin on one half of the head yellowed and purpled, its surface at points having shredded off to form stringy, extruding lengths around the right ear. The face looked twisted and rickety, as if one plate of a vice had been secured on the crest of the brow and the other tightened on the bottom of the chin and the two plates had then been wrenched horizontally an inch in opposite directions, rendering the bone symmetry all skew-whiff, about ten degrees out of true. The shoulders also bowed and sloped at an ungainly angle. His right hand had fallen open with a kitchen knife still resting in its fingers, two of which were visibly sticking out of a damaged white synthetic glove.

Slim broke the silence in the most ponderous tone of meditation of which he was capable, apostrophising the corpse directly in what Nesbit may perhaps have been able to diagnose as a stab at Shakespearean tragedy, Act V, final scene.

"What are we going to do with you, eh?"[39]

When McNamara came to with the sounds and smells of a hospital around him, it was in the ambit of overheard voices. He recognised Nesbit's and did not open his eyes. The other speaker was a woman.

"When?" Nesbit said.

"Not before I have been able to examine him once he is conscious," the woman said. "There is evidence of a stroke whose severity we don't yet know. Until I see what condition he is in, you'll have to wait. The time window for reversing the damage in many kinds of

[39] Despite the typical Clockmaniac snideness here, this is a suitably pentameter, if only half iambic, line. Moreover, the inclusive or royal "we" is often deployed in the closing declamation by whatever minor character has been shuffled onto Shakespeare's stage to wind things up with windy banalities (cf. "We shall not spend a large expense of time/Before we reckon with your several loves" etc. etc. These particular two lines are nothing but uncontrolled afflatus elongating a tragic play which is exiguously on the short side. They could easily be rendered as one: "It won't be long until I thank you all.")

stroke is hours. And it's not as if he is going anywhere."

The two interlocutors seemed to melt away and McNamara drifted off again. Later in the day he woke once more and the welcome, still bandaged and braced head of William Stoner was regarding him from the side of the bed.

"You came to see me for a longer visit this time, old boy?" Stoner said with a little artificial glee.

McNamara made to respond but his tongue and lips did not move. All that came out was a throaty grunt.

It became clear to both of them after a few more remarks of Stoner's that speech from McNamara was not on the current agenda. He tried to move his right arm but it hung limply on top of the bed sheet. So he called his left arm into life while pinching its thumb and forefinger together and wiggling them in the air. Stoner went to get a paper and pen. When he returned with a nurse he laid them gently on McNamara's midriff while the patient's bed was raised to a reclining position.

McNamara stared at the little lined notepad in his lap. It slid to the side and fell off the bed. His reflexive attempt to stop it doing so with his right hand had entirely failed.

The nurse scrabbled for the paper and placed it again before McNamara, who nodded feebly and put the nib of the pen towards the white surface. Then he stopped. What were they, those shapes one drew to represent sounds? He could not find the word for them but he knew it began with a ... and then he could not remember the letter it began with. There were a couple of dozen of those shapes but every child learned them young. He sort of remembered remembering them in a certain kind of order. How did it begin again? But that he could not at this moment recall.

He could, however, hear and understand Stoner and everyone else perfectly well. Eventually Stoner twigged and proposed a one-grunt-for-yes, two-grunts-for-no, three-grunts-for-don't-know system.

"You can't speak?" Stoner asked.

McNamara gave a double grunt.

"Can you write?"

The same response came. Stoner picked up the paper and scribbled something and put it before him. When McNamara looked at it, it said, "Can you read?" This made him excited and he grunted once and nodded his head and waggled his left index finger enthusiastically at the page. There were those shapes he remembered...

When Nesbit arrived again the doctor continued to make things difficult for him.

"Dysphasia?" Nesbit repeated querulously.

"In the case of Professor McNamara, inability to speak or write, but we have discovered that he can listen and read perfectly well. In other words, he is passively receptive to language but cannot actively produce it. I have him booked in for a CT scan in an hour, which will tell us the full extent of his trauma, but it will almost certainly be a haemorrhage in the left hemisphere of the brain. In most cases like this the patient improves, if at all, only after some weeks or months of therapy. It all depends on the severity."

"If at all?" Nesbit complained. "Weeks or months?"

"Well," the doctor went on, "as I said before, he's not going anywhere soon. So I suggest you check in again in a while and I'll let you know how he's doing."

Nesbit retreated and disappeared back to the depths of Buckinghamshire, emanating a trail of disgruntled bad feeling.

As they wheeled him through the corridors to the CT scan room, McNamara reflected that it was his long-term memory that was foggy. He remembered recent events very well. He knew that Buckrack was dead. He remembered pulling aside the sliding door of the wardrobe and seeing the American's slumped, dis-coloured, misshapen body. And he knew that it was almost certainly the double hammer blow to the American's head which had, if only eventually, finished him off. As the scanning machine slowly took multiple images of his own altered brain, he had time rather to congratulate himself. He had despatched a serial murderer. McNamara did not at this moment conceive of himself as a murderer. Nor did it occur to him that the deaths of Asterisk and two CIA agents, not to speak of fellow hospital inmate Stoner's being bodily assaulted with half a brick, had any consequential connection with his having whacked Buckrack into the middle of the next life with that handy meat tenderizer.

On the gurney-journey back to the ward it occurred to him that there was absolutely none of the customary pain in his back. To think that he had once hypo-chondriacally fantasised this as potential cancer of the pancreas!

Stoner returned to his bedside towards nightfall, this time with Redman. They sat on either side of him and played a jolly game of twenty closed-ended questions. They managed to keep it so light-hearted and natural-seeming that all three of them almost convinced themselves for the time being that everything was totally normal and nothing ultimately devastating had taken place.

McNamara wondered once or twice where Drusilla was but none of the questions mentioned her, so he received no enlightenment, and was unable to ask. But he had a nagging intuition that he might never see her again.

Of course, the University of Odium died too. It was so fatally weakened that it could not ride the third colossal wave of public opprobium and infamy to tower over it in a single year.

The Minister of State for Universities, Science, Research and Innovation stepped in to throw a spanner in the works of the always fired-up media circus as soon as it began erecting its tent.[40] She established what was termed an "inquiry". This sounded official and pukka to everyone who heard the word used to describe it on Radio 4 (which announced it with all the authority of a ringmaster introducing the next act), but it actually consisted of the Minister sending one unidentified but governmentally authorised man or woman or person of indeterminate sex to Odium, who met briefly with Elfyn Dethbridge and said, "You are in charge now. Sort it out." This anonymous person then left Odium and immediately travelled north to the city of Surleighwick, where s/he/they/it/ze met the Vice Chancellor of its University and informed him, "You have permission fully to incorporate the University of Odium. Our guy there is Elfyn Dethbridge. Tell him what to do." Having issued this ordinance, the said official returned to Whitehall and wrote an unsigned thirty-five-page document which was forwarded for formal approval to a Parliamentary committee, and approved.

[40] "OVERWHELMING DEATHS IMMOBILISE USELESS MASTERMINDS" spelled out *The Sun* in its first ever acrostic headline.

Elfyn Dethbridge, who was about as knowledgeable of how the real world worked as the Elfyn Dethbridge on the desert island of Robert McNamara's favourite joke about him, did as he was told. He enlarged and completed the already launched redundancy process with the merciless thoroughness of a driver stopping and reversing to make sure a hedgehog is dead. By September the University of Odium existed no more. New entrants there would be welcomed to the University of Surleighwick, Odium Campus (USOC).[41] The expectation was that a change of nomenclature would make everything terrible that had taken place somehow rapidly be forgotten. And largely, in the way that a reader concludes one novel rather speedily in order to launch immediately into another, it was.

But not by James Redman. He bore the burden of

---

[41] Those of us in present-day institutions of higher learning (so high that we exist exclusively in The Cloud, like my own Booleshire University) often struggle with this antiquated, geographically situated notion of the university as a physical entity with buildings, land, a postcode, and academics and students who actually once met in contiguous spaces and temporalities. The entire Odium trilogy, indeed, is largely an object of contemporary interest because it is the very last gasp in the genre of the "campus novel" of the analogue epoch in which learning was conducted by means of discursive exchange between actual physical bodies in real time. No one now, in 2084, could cobble such an eventful narrative out of higher education, which these days is effected entirely by remote communicational means, which relies (in our inventive marketing language) on "no campus other than the hippocampus", and which in the precise sciences is entirely robotised; all of which renders impossible the gross interpersonal shenanigans which we witness in Clockman's historically notable (if artistically and morally deprecable) epic.

the history of the University of Odium, but also transmitted it to future ages, in a very personal way. His
employment was (like Avril Poon's) terminated as part
of Dethbridge's massacre. When, a few weeks later, the
Welshman was appointed as the new Registrar of
USOC, Redman leaked to the media the video of him
having kinky sex with a macho young Spaniard which
had somehow found its way onto McNamara's mobile
phone. This made the University of Surleighwick think
twice, and it quietly erased Dethbridge from its payroll.
He was never heard of again. Even in Brighton.

Over the summer, Redman moved McNamara out of
the hospital into his house at 111 Maryland Lane, where
he tended to him selflessly throughout a long recovery
that resulted in the stricken man regaining the power of
writing but not of speech. They came to form an odd
couple, the joined-at-the-hip double act he had once
denied they were, surviving amply on Redman's carer's
allowance and McNamara's disability living allowance
and pension, sharing the reading of books and the
gluttonous consumption of American TV series like a
pair of companionable male spinsters. Both secretly
considered these the finest, most peaceful years of their
conflict-ridden lives. They also came to agree that a
womanless existence tends to minimise the pains of
men growing towards agedness.

William Stoner died attached to a ventilator in the
same hospital a month into the Covid pandemic of
2020. So did McNamara a few weeks later. His last
thought was, "Who the hell did Drusilla have sex with
on her final day?" (He had read and re-read the post-
mortem report more times than he could count.) But by
then, using his own and McNamara's personal
knowledge, and the copious electronic records they had

both preserved from their employment, Redman had written and secured an agent for his first ever book, a five-hundred-page doorstopper called *The Fall of the University of Odium: the Inside Story*. A bidding war among publishers ensued; it was serialised in *The Sunday Times* and *The Washington Post*, its revelations of CIA involvement in serial murder on British soil making it a sensational bestseller on both sides of the pond and giving the newly elected President Biden yet another stick with which to beat Donald Trump. The two salient facts it did not reveal were the two things Redman and McNamara had never confessed to each other, namely that the former had cuckolded the latter and that the latter had murdered Cannon Buckrack. Amazon adapted it as a highly successful mini-series in 2022. Redman's bank account filled to overflowing with much wanted liquidity from many tributary streams.

Unfortunately for everyone, three years later, so did the North Sea. The Arctic ice pack lost its long patience with world governments not taking it seriously and decided to teach humanity a cold hard lesson. It cleaved in twain and pushed a fifth of its mass gently south into the Norwegian Sea. This warmed it up sufficiently to render it into vast icebergs which were then funneled into the North Sea, which heated the gargantuan masses of ice even more, especially just south of Aberdeen, resulting in the flatlands of east-coastal Britain and west-coastal Europe being entirely engulfed in ice-cold tsunamis which permanently raised the sea level by over a hundred feet. Most of Holland, Belgium and Northern France were entirely submerged. From just south of Edinburgh to the south coast of England, the largely flat eastern seaboard of Britain became an archipelago of rare peaks which had been turned into marooned islands.

Detective Superintendent Nesbit, who lived in a pleasant four-bedroomed detached house in the Chiltern Hills, survived. He had been promoted to Chief Superintendent a few weeks before. But his work dried up in direct proportion to how very wet and thus empty of criminals his county generally became. Those who did not perish in the Great Flood fled to what remained of Britain, and so did he, outcome unrecorded.

Likewise, no one knows what fate befell Chivers.

It is well known, on the other hand, that Alice Dean became the first ever signing deaf person to assume a senior position in government (she was to be a long-serving Minister of State for Education), and is double-handedly responsible for ensuring that British Sign Language is now taught in all state schools and that no video is permitted to be circulated without subtitles. When she appeared on *Desert Island Discs* (largely guided by an impulse to self-demonstrate that Radio 4 needed to clean up its act and be more inclusive towards deaf people) she named James Redman as her personal role model of the decent human being.

Continuous British mainland now started only west of a wiggly line drawn from Newcastle through Leeds and Bristol to Exeter: essentially the ancient Celtic territories and a jagged remnant of the north of England. Redman was spared the need to join the exodus because he had earlier purchased an opulent six-bedroomed retreat in mid-Wales on the back of his authorial bounty, and was at last tasting the joys of domestic luxury which he had privately envied in McNamara as Vice Chancellor. But this did not save him. In late 2025 he was immolated in a calamitously destructive arson attack on his property carried out by

Welsh nationalists who had risen up against the hordes of English refugees who had invaded their homeland. His bodily ashes were scattered in the Cambrian Mountains by natural, breezy means.

With London and Birmingham literally wiped off the map, and Edinburgh too close to the North Sea for comfort, the British Parliament removed to Glasgow. The West Country, now an island, declared political autonomy in 2026, and was not opposed, its move rather spurring the Scots and the Welsh subsequently to render themselves independent of each other also (the near-extinction of the Conservative Party in consecutive general elections made this a mere Parliamentary formality). What remained of England was accorded intermediate principality status by the two larger nations, which eventually made a treaty absorbing its contiguous territories into theirs, so that by 2035 what had been Britain was now a massively enlarged Scotland (slightly bigger than the size of old England), an appreciably extended Wales (now almost as large as Ireland), and the Independent People's Republic of Wessex (basically Cornwall, Devon and what was left of Somerset and Dorset).

All three of these polities became mountingly, radically socialistic. They were thus viewed very warily from the now much more distant European continent, somewhat in the way that the United States viewed Castro's Cuba, and in Berlin and Rome and Madrid people consoled themselves that the divide first created by Brexit had in these latter days been made absolutely unbridgeable by the enormous stretch of dismal water now known as The Gulf of Europa.

In Odium, all that remained was the hill on which the University had grown, peaked by what had hitherto been McNamara's house and what had once been called the Trump Building. To get to it you had to take a boat from a city fourteen miles to the west on the coastal edge of the Bay of East Wales, yet many thousands of people did so every year. Because Redman's book and the resultant Amazon series had made it so globally famous, the state-owned National Trust bought the functionless island from the rapidly virtualising University of Surleighwick and turned it into a profitable visitor attraction. It was often compared to Alcatraz, but was generally considered to be much more edifying. As a spectacle it was dramatically enlivened by an inert population of five thousand life-sized human figures representing past students and staff. Tourists could lodge in the halls of residence and imaginatively relive the quaint experience of a campus-based education, wander through lecture halls thronged with stationary undergraduates cast in wax in roped-off tiered seating, or see them bent over scientific experiments in the original laboratories, or leafing through actual paper books in the lovingly preserved library stacks. Most popular of all was the Vice Chancellor's abode, where people flocked as they still do in the Palace of Holy-roodhouse to the very spot where David Rizzio was murdered by trespassing rebels in 1566, to see the grisly cellar in which Drusilla Frost had the life choked out of her, before proceeding upstairs to the bedroom, where had been installed a waxwork tableau vivant showing Vice Chancellor Robert McNamara staring in terror and alarm at the incipiently putrefying carcass of the notorious American serial killer, Cannon Buckrack, revealed in the walk-in wardrobe, thence up a tiny spiral passageway to any of the four turrets that castellated the house, to gaze south-east across the sea and marvel that the nearest piece of continuous dry land in a straight line was Germany.

But even the tasteful theme park or still-life theatre or static fiction that the one-time University of Odium had become could not endure. Entropy stalks the universe. Decay ultimately infects all. Erosion gnaws until its destructive urge is consummated. Even earth does not abide. The salt sea, ever washing into the caves at the base of the stranded Holm of Odium (as it had come to be called), with each relentless stroke insinuating itself deeper inside the weak chalky foundations, turning them gradually to pulp, then to paste, then into a perilous puree, contrived for it a last, memorable fall.

No one died when its 693,940,207,425 tons of ancient geological matter collapsed on Michaelmas Day, 2047 (a date ironically close to that on which students used to arrive there for the beginning of their academic year) and left a vast smear of earth drifting on the waves, which the sea slowly absorbed into itself in the weeks that followed. The Holm had been declared unsafe and abandoned for over a year by then. It was considered so dangerous that the National Trust had not dared even to venture there to recover all its installed touristic paraphernalia. Five thousand wax-work students and academics, and one serial murderer in effigy, along with an estimated 150,000 yellowed library books, therefore floated pollutingly out into the grey liquid expanse. A single male human skeleton was also discovered during the salvage operation, its limbs intertwined somewhat obscenely with a staring waxen simulacrum of a female Indian student it seemed to be using as a kind of raft, which discovery fuelled social media speculation that perhaps there had once been yet another unsolved murder at the University of Odium. These rumours did not cease with the eventual identification of the bones as those of the prophetic Professor Adrian Plumb.

THE END

"The novel that simply cries out to be a TV mini-series ... the *House of Cards* of the modern British university ... a thrilling satirical exposure of the witless evils of today's academy."

TV FOR TOMORROW

"Clockman has done it again! It's all here: the obloquy which taints all who choose to serve in today's university; the tyranny of social media; Brexit; the banal realities of modern anti-terrorism; even a zombie and ripe evidence that the #MeToo movement is an understatement. I laughed all the way through then wrote my resignation letter."

T(R)OPICAL LITERATURE

"At last Clockman's great comic trilogy is concluded. Quentin Tarantino meets the campus novel in an ecstatic renovation of the genre. Gone is all the humanistic twaddle and intellectual imposture which have beset the depiction of universities in fiction since day one. In their place we get the modern institution in all its cold-blooded malice, mean-spirited calculation, narrow-minded prejudice and, ultimately, maniacal self-destructiveness."

PSYCHOTEXTE

Now available in one volume as *The Odium Trilogy*